Emma Orczy

THE EMPEROR'S CANDLESTICKS
(A Spy Classic)

OK Publishing 2021

Emma Orczy
THE EMPEROR'S CANDLESTICKS

(A Spy Classic)

Published by
MUSAICUM
Books

- Advanced Digital Solutions & High-Quality book Formatting -

musaicumbooks@okpublishing.info

2021 OK Publishing

ISBN 978-80-272-7817-6

Contents

Chapter I

GAY, chic Vienna was *en fête*. What would you? Shrove Tuesday is the very last day, allowed by our Holy Mother the Church for revelry, before the long austere forty days of Lent, and if we do not make use of her full permission to enjoy ourselves, to the full extent of out capacity, we shall have nothing left to atone for to-morrow, when the good fathers place the cross of ashes on our foreheads, and bid us remember that dust we are, to dust return.

Therefore Vienna was drinking the overflowing cup of pleasure to-day; had been drinking in it in its gaily lighted streets and boulevards, and was now enjoying its last drops at the opera ball, the climax to a carnival that had been unusually brilliant this year.

And in the hall, where but two nights ago the harmonious discords of Wagner's "Niebelungen" had enchanted and puzzled a seriously-minded audience, to-night Pierrots and Pierrettes, Fausts and Marguerites, nymphs, fairies, gnomes and what-nots chased each other with merry cries and loud laughter, to the sweet tunes of Strauss' melodious, dreamy waltzes; while the boxes, each filled with spectators eager to watch, though afraid to mingle in the giddy throng, showed mysterious dominoes and black masks, behind which gleamed eyes rendered bright with suppressed excitement at the intoxicating spectacle below.

"Come down, fair domino, I know thee," whispered a richly dressed odalisque, whose jewelled mask could not outshine the merry twinkle of her black eyes beneath. She had placed one dainty hand on the ledge of a pit tier box, in which two black dominoes had sat for some time, partially hidden by the half-drawn curtains, and had watched the gay throng beneath them for some half-hour or so, apparently unnoticed.

The taller of the two dominoes bent forward, trying to pierce the enterprising houri's disguise.

"Nay! if you know me, fair mask, come up to me, and let me renew an acquaintance that should have never been dropped!"

But she had once more disappeared as swiftly as she had come, and the black domino, whose curiosity was aroused, tried vainly to distinguish her graceful figure among the glitter of the moving crowd.

"I wonder our sober dresses succeeded in drawing that gay butterfly's attention," he said, turning to his companion, "and what her object was in speaking to me, if she did not mean to continue the *causerie*."

"Oh, it is the usual way with these gay Viennese *bourgeoisies*," replied his companion; "your Imperial Highness has been sitting too much in the shade of that curtain, and the odalisque thought your obvious desire to remain hidden an object of interest."

The taller domino now lent forward in the box, his opera-glass glued to his mask, eagerly scanning the crowd; but, though numerous Moorish and Turkish veiled figures passed backwards and forwards, he did not recognise the enterprising odalisque among them.

"Look not for the good that lies far away when the best is so close at hand," whispered a mocking voice, close to his elbow.

The black domino turned sharply round, just in time to catch hold of a little hand, which had crept round the column, that separated the box in which he was sitting, from the adjoining one.

"The best is still too far," he whispered; "is it unattainable?"

"Always try to obtain the best," replied the mocking voice, "even at the risk of scaling the inaccessible walls of an opera-box."

"I cannot get to thee, fair mask, without momentarily letting go this tiny hand, and it is never safe to let a bird, even for a moment, out of its cage."

"Black Domino, we often must risk the lesser to obtain the great," said the odalisque maliciously.

"I entreat your Imperial Highness to remain here," said the second domino imploringly; "you are here incognito: I am the only one in attendance on you Highness, and ——"

"All the more reason why it should be possible, for one brief moment, for a Tsarevitch to do as he likes," retorted the taller domino laughingly.

And, before his companion had time to add another word of warning, the young man had, with the freedom which King Carnival always allows at such a time and in such places, climbed the ledge of the box, and scrambled with youthful alacrity into the one that contained his mysterious bright-eyed houri.

But alas! for the waywardness and fickleness of the daughters of the East, no sooner had the black domino safely reached *terra firma* once more, after his perilous climb, than the swift opening and shutting of a door told him but too plain that the will-o'-the-wisp wished to evade him yet again.

What young man is there, be him prince or peasant, who would have allowed so mocking a game to be carried on at his expense. Nicholas Alexandrovitch, son and heir to the Tsar of all Russias, remembered only that he was twenty years of age, that he had come to the opera ball, accompanied by that dry old stick Lavrovski, with the sole purpose of enjoying himself incognito for once, and...he started off in hot pursuit.

The passage behind the box was quite empty, but in the direction leading to the *foyer*, some fifty yards, distant, he distantly caught the sight of a swiftly disappearing figure, and the heels of the prettiest pair of Turkish slippers it had ever been his good fortune to see.

The *foyer* was, at that late hour of the night, a scene of the most motley, most picturesque confusion. Assyrian queens were walking arm in arm with John Bulls, Marguerites were co-quetting unblushingly with gallants of some two centuries later, while Hamlets and Orthellos were indulging in the favourite Viennese pastime of hoisting their present partners on to the tallest pillars they could find, with a view to starving them out up there, into a jump some ten or twelve feet below, when they would perforce land into the outstretched arms of their delighted swains.

And very pretty these tall pillars looked, thus decorated with living, laughing, chatting figures of v Ivándières, Pierrettes-ay, and of sober Ophelias and languishing Isoldes. But the black domino heeded than not; darting hither and thither, taking no notice of cheeky sallies and rough *bousculades*, he pushed his way through the crowd towards one spot, close to the entrance, where a special little jewelled cap was fast disappearing through the wide open portals, that led into the gaily lighted place beyond.

The odalisque had evidently either repented of her audacious adventure, or was possessed of an exceptionally bold spirit, for without a moment's hesitation she ran down the stone steps, taking no further heed of the jesting crowd she was forced to pass through, or of the two or three idle masks who accosted her, and also started in pursuit.

Having reached the bottom of the steps she seemed to hesitate a moment, only a second perhaps-was it intentionally?-but that second gave Nicholas Alexandrovitch the chance he had for some time striven for; he overtook her, just as she laid her hand on the door of a *fiaker* which has drawn up, and lifting her off the ground as if she were a feather, he placed her inside, and sat down in front of her, hot and panting, while the coachman, without apparently waiting for any directions, drove off rapidly through the ever noisier and gayer crowd.

Chapter II

ALL this had excited little or no attention among the bystanders. How should it? An opera ball teems with such episodes.

Two young people, one in pursuit of the other–a signal–a handy *fiaker, et voilà!* Who cares? Everybody is busy with his own affairs, his own little bits of adventure and intrigue.

Surely that grey domino over there, standing under one of the fine electric light chandeliers, could have no interest in the unknown odalisque and her ardent swain, for he made not the slightest attempt at pursuit; yet his eyes followed the fast disappearing *fiaker*, as long as it was recognisable amidst the crowd of vehicles and mummers. A young man he was; evidently not anxious to remain incognito, for he had thrown back the hood of his domino, and held the mask in his hand.

Yet though he thus, as it were, courted recognition, he visibly started as a soft musical voice, with the faintest vestige of foreign intonation, addressed him merrily.

"Why so moody, M. Volenski? Have Strauss' waltzes tired out your spirits, or has your donna eloped with a hated rival?"

The young man pulled himself together, and forced open his eyes and thoughts to wander away from the *fiaker*, which now appeared as a mere speck, to the graceful figure in front of him, who owned that musical voice and had called him by name.

"Madam Demidoff!" he said, evidently not pleasantly surprised.

"Herself," she replied, laughingly; "do not assume an astonishment, so badly justified. I am not a Viennese *grande dame*, and coming to an opera ball is not the most unpardonable of my eccentricities."

"Yes! but alone?"

"Not alone," she rejoined, still merry, "since you are here to protect me from my worst perils, and lend me a helping hand in the most dire difficulties."

"Allow me to start on these most enviable functions by finding your carriage for you," he said, a trifle absently.

She bit her lip, and tried a laugh, but this time there was a *soupçon* of harshness in the soft foreign notes.

"Ah, Iván, how you must reckon on my indulgence, that you venture so unguardedly on so ungallant a speech!"

"Was it ungallant?"

"Come, what would your judgement be on a young man, one of our *jeunesse dorée*, who, meeting a lady at the opera ball, offers, after the first two minutes, to find her carriage for her."

"I should deem it to be an unpardonable sin, and punishable by some nameless tortures, if that lady happens to be Madam Demidoff," he said, striving to make banal speeches to hide his evident desire for immediate retreat.

She looked at his keenly for a minute, then sighed a quick, impatient little sigh.

"Well, call my carriage, Iván; I will not keep you, you obviously have some pressing engagement."

"The Cardinal —- " he began clumsily.

"Ah! his Eminence requires your attention at so late an hour?" she said, still a little bitterly.

"his Eminence is leaving Vienna to-morrow and there are still many letters to answer. I shall probably be writing most of the night through."

She appeared content with this explanation, and while Volenski gave directions to one of the gorgeous attendants stationed outside the house to call Madam Demidoff's carriage, she resumed the conversation in a more matter-of-fact tone.

"his Eminence will be glad of a holiday after the trying diplomatic business of the past few weeks; and you, M. Volenski, I feel sure have also earned a few days repose.

"The Cardinal certainly has given me two or three weeks' respite, while he himself goes to Tyrol for the benefit of his health."

"And after that?"

"We meet at Petersburg, where his Eminence has an important memorial to submit to his Majesty the Tsar."

"You yourself, madame —- "

"Yes, I shall probably be there before you both arrive, and thus have the honour of welcoming his Eminence in person. But here is my carriage. It is 'au revoir,' then, M. Volenski, not 'adieu,' luckily for you," she added once more coquettishly, "for had it been a longer parting I should have found it hard to forgive your not even calling to leave a bit of pasteboard with my concierge."

He had given her his arm, and was leading her down the wide stone stairs, trying all the while not to appear relieved that the interview was at last over, and his faro companion on the way to leaving him alone with his anxieties and agitation.

"Good-night, Iván," she said, after her had helped her into her carriage, and wrapped her furs round her.

Long after her coachman had started she leant her head out of the window, and watched him, as long as she could distinguish his grey domino among the crowd; there was a wistful look on her face, also a frown, perhaps of self contempt. Then, when the carriage had left the opera house, with all its gaiety and tumult, behind, and she no longer could see Iván Volenski's figure at the foot of the wide stone stairs, she seemed to dismiss with an impatient sigh and a shrug any little touch of sentiment that may have lurked in her thoughts, and it was an impassive, slightly irritable *grande dame* who alighted out of the little elegant *coupé*, under the portico of one of the finest houses on the Kolowrátring.

"Send Eugen to me in my boudoir at once," she said to the footmen, who preceded her upstairs. "If he is from home, one of you sit up till he comes in; if he is asleep, he must be wakened forthwith."

She seemed too agitated to sit down, though the arm-chairs in her luxurious boudoir stood most invitingly by. She was pacing up and down the room, listening for every footstep. Far from her was all touch of sentiment, all recollection of the figure in the grey domino whom she had called Iván, and who seemed all but too eager to be rid of her.

What she had seen to-night, not half hour ago, had mystified her beyond expression. She (and of this she felt convinced), was the only person, with the exception of old Count Lavrovski, and the one confidential valet, who, in this city, knew that in the guise of that black domino was the heir to the Russian throne.

He had been spoken to by a forward masque, disguised as an odalisque; that was neither surprising nor unusual at carnival time, when every description of forwardness is not only permissible, but encouraged. The Tsarevitch, with youthful impetuosity, had followed, forgetting his rank and the dangers that always surround his position, and both he and the odalisque had disappeared into a *fiaker*, which Madame Demidoff felt convinced had been there ready waiting for them, and driven off, without apparently any directions being given to the coachman.

"Come in,!" she said, much relieved, as a discreet footstep, and a rap at the door caught her ear, still on the alert. She took up a cigarette from a little case that lay close to her hand; she felt it would calm her nerves, and steady her voice.

A man entered-flat-nosed, high cheek-boned Russian of the lower classes, whose low forehead betokened an absence of what is usually called intellectuality, but whose piercing, cold, grey eyes, deeply sunk between the thinnest of lids, spoke of cunning and alacrity. A useful man, no doubt. Madame Demidoff seemed more calm the moment she spoke to him.

"Eugen," she said, "listen to me, for something very mysterious has happened at the opera ball to-night, and there is some work you must do for me now, at once, and also during the course of to-morrow.

"The Tsarevitch went to the opera ball to-night disguised as a black domino.... Yes! he was in Vienna.... Incognito.... No one knew it.... The whole thing was foolish in the extreme, and I am beginning to fear some foul agency must have been at work, he was decoyed from his opera-box by a woman dressed as an odalisque... in red and gold, I think...no matter the description...

There were hundreds in that guise at the opera. Nicholas Alexandrovitch followed her; a *fiaker* was waiting for them; he jumped in, and it drove off at great rapidity towards the old town."

"Yes, *barina?*"

For she had paused a moment to collect her thoughts before giving him her final directions.

"You must find out for me first whether the Tsarevitch has returned to his hotel, and if not, what steps Count Lavrovski is taking to discover the key to the mystery. You must dog the old man's every footstep, and if he goes to the police, or sends any telegraphic message across to Petersburg, you must apprise me of it at once. Moreover, both outside the opera house, at the *fiaker* stations, ands at the various railways, you must glean what scraps of information you can relating to the flying odalisque and domino, or the *fiaker* that drove them. I leave by the express for Petersburg to-morrow at midnight; you must come and tell me what you have learnt in the early part of the evening."

She dismissed him now, and when once more alone she sat and thought over the occurrences of to-night. Then it was that and anon the wistful look-almost of yearning, that rendered her aristocratic face so sweet and tender-crept into her eyes; but when it came, the impatient little sigh and self-contemptuous frown invariably accompanied it. Surely this worldly woman, this elegant *grande dame*, would not allow even the faintest vestige of sentiment to creep up among her recollections of the gay carnival ball, more especially as that sentiment was evidently directed towards one who ——-

"Ah me!" Madame Demidoff sighed again, threw away her cigarette, and rang for her maid, all with the idea of putting an end to any more thinking that night.

Chapter III

As soon as Iván Volenski lost sight completely of Madame Demidoff's carriage, he, with a sigh of relief, retraced his steps up the wide stairs of the opera house, and joined a couple of dominoes, who, dressed like himself in uniform grey, stood isolated among the groups of masks that encumbered the entrance to the *foyer*. Together all three began sauntering in the direction of the Kolowátring.

They walked on in silence for some time, smoking cigarettes and pushing their way through the crowd as best they could.

On the Ringstrasse the scene was as gay as ever; laughing groups of masks in bands of a score or so occupying the whole width of the street made progress somewhat difficult. But the three grey dominoes seemed in no great hurry; they exchanged jests where repartee was expected of them, and mixed with the crowd where it was impossible to avoid it.

The sumptuous houses and gorgeously decorated shops on either side were illuminated with many coloured lights, changing this midnight hour into light as broad as day. On the balconies, gaily festooned with flowers, groups of onlookers gazed on the animated scene below, whilst every now and then, from some opened windows, dreamy waltzes and weird *csárdás* mingled with the noisy street cries and laughter, telling of aristocratic balls and parties, where the King Carnival was courted with equal mirth if somewhat less exuberance and noise. Sometimes the groups of mummers would stop beneath some of these windows and watch the bejewelled figures flitting to-and-fro, and listen to the soft cadences of the gipsy music-the one thing Hungarian, the Viennese cannot bring themselves to despise.

But the three dominoes did not pause long, amidst this gay and bustling scene, nor did the brilliant lighted Ring appear to have any attraction for them, for presently they turned into a side street, uninviting and dark though it seemed; and being free to walk more rapidly, soon left the sounds of merry laughter and revelry far behind them.

Still they walked on in silence, not heeding now the few muffled masks that passed them with a laugh and jest, on their way towards the gayer part of the city.

With these few exceptions the streets they now crossed were completely deserted; no illuminations from the windows proclaimed the reign of King Carnival, no sound of dreamy waltz music lent a touch of merriment to the dismal, stone-paved courtyards that yawned drearily on either side.

Into one of these the three dominoes presently turned, and, with out waiting to reply to the *concierge's* challenge as to whom they were seeking at so late an hour, they found their way to the back stone staircase, which was but dimly lighted by a hanging lamp, that flickered in the draught, and threw weird shadows on the steps. Having reached the second flight, one of the dominoes gave a peculiar rhythmic knock on one of the doors facing him, which after a few moments was thrown open, while an anxious voice asked:

"Is that you, Baloukine?"

"Yes," replied the domino, "with Iván and Serge; let us in."

The room which they had now entered, furnished with an attempt at comfort, half as an office, and half as a smoking lounge, was filled with some twelve or fourteen men, of all ages, and apparently, judging from their clothes, of very mixed social positions; while four or five of them, collarless, and probably shirtless, wore working jackets and clumsy boots, some wore beautifully cut dress-clothes and spotless linen, with a flower in the button-hole, and one elderly man, with a pointed grey beard, and handsome, aristocratic features, wore two or three decorations fastened to his coat.

All, however, whether peer or peasant, seemed on the best of terms together, and smoking pipes and cigarettes of peace and fraternity.

"What news?" asked half a dozen voices, as the new arrivals divested themselves of their grey dominoes, and shook hands with those sitting around.

"The best."

"Where is he?" asked a voice.

"In Mirkovitch's *fiaker* with Maria Stefanowna."

"And presently?"

"Mirkovitch's guest at No 21, Heumarkt."

The questions and answers followed each other in rapid succession; the tension of suspense had evidently been great, the relief at the news most obviously welcome, for a sigh of satisfaction seemed to rise in unison from a dozen heaving, oppressed chests.

"And Mirkovitch?" asked one of the older men.

"He will be here anon."

"As soon as *he* is safe under lock and key."

"Then he is in our power?"

"Absolutely."

"Did Lavrovski attempt to follow him?

"Not till it was too late, and the *fiaker* out of sight. He fell into the trap, without a shadow of suspicion."

There was a pause now; evidently much had to be thought of and serious points considered, for during the next ten minutes not a sound disturbed the stillness of the room, save the crackling of burning logs in the wide chimney, and one or two whispered questions and rapidly given answers.

Then a heavy tread was heard in the passage outside, the same rhythmical knock on the door, while a gruff voice said:

"Mirkovitch."

A Herculean man, some six foot three in height, with long grey hair thrown back from a massive forehead, and piecing grey eyes, half-hidden under a pair of bushy eyebrows, now joined the group of smokers, greeting them all but with two words:

"All safe."

"Prisoner?"

"Safely in my house; no windows, only a skylight. No chance of discovery, and less of escape."

"And Maria Stefenowna?"

"Did her part splendidly; he suspected nothing till he heard the door locked behind him."

"Did he speak?"

"Only to call himself a fool, which remark was obvious."

"He asked no questions?"

"None."

"The deaf-mute valet was there to receive him?"

"Yes, and waited on him, while he took some of the supper we has prepared for him."

"What about Lavrovski?" asked a voice from the further end of the room.

"He went back to his box, and is waiting there now, I should imagine."

"In the meanwhile, Mirkovitch, you have promised us the best treatment for our prisoner."

"Yes," said Mirkovitch grimly. "I hate him, but I will treat him well. The deaf-mute is a skilled valet, the rooms are comfortable, the bad is luxurious, the food will be choice and plentiful. Very different," he added sullenly, "from what Denajewski and the others are enduring at this moment."

"They are practically free now," said a young voice enthusiastically; "we can demand their liberty; let them refuse it, if they dare."

"Yes," added Mirkovitch with a smile, "it would go hard with Nicholas Alexandrovitch now if they refused to let our comrades go."

"To business, friends, there is no time for talk," said the authoritative voice of the elderly man who wore decoration.

The cigarettes and pipes were with one accord put aside, and all chairs turned towards to the table placed in the centre of the room, on which stood a tempered with a green shade, and scattered all about, loose bundles of paper, covered with writings and signatures.

"There are many points to decide," resumed he, who appeared to be a leader amongst them; "the deed, accomplished to-night, thanks to those heads who planned, and those arms who executed it, great as it is, has still a greater object in view. This, we over here cannot attain; the turn of Taraniew and the brothers in Petersburg has now come, to do their share of the work."

The chairman paused, all heads nodded in acquiescence, then he resumed:

"We have been obliged to act very hurriedly and on our own initiative. Taraniew and the others, so far, know absolutely nothing."

"They must hear of it at once," said one voice.

"And cease any plotting of their own," assented another.

"It could only now lead to certain disaster," agreed the chairman, "if they were in any sort of way to draw the attention of the Third Section on themselves."

"Or us!" grimly added Mirkovitch.

"Obviously, therefore, our messenger's duty to them will be twofold," said the president. "The bringing of great news, as it now stands, and our instructions as to the next course they must follow to attain the noble object we all have in view."

"Yes, the letter to Alexander III," said a young voice eagerly.

This was the important point; more eagerness in the listeners, more enthusiasm among the younger men was, if possible, discernible.

"I have here," said the president, taking a document from the table, "with the help of the committee, embodied our idea as to how that letter should be framed."

"It will be an appetising breakfast relish for the autocrat of all the Russians when he finds it, as he does all our written warnings, underneath his cup of morning coffee," sneered Mirkovitch, who had been sitting all this while smoking grimly, and muttering at intervals short sentences between his teeth, which boded no good to the prisoner he had under his charge.

"Our letter," said the president, "this time will contain the information that the Tsarevitch is, at the present moment, in the hands of some persons unknown, and that those persons will continue to hold him a hostage till certain conditions are complied with."

"Those conditions being?" queried one of the bystanders.

"Complete pardon for Dunajewski, and all those who are in prison with him in connection with that lat plot, together with a free pass out of the country."

"Nicholas Alexandrovitch to be set free the day they have crossed the frontier," added a member of the committee.

"If in answer to this he simply sets the Third Section on our track?" queried a voice diffidently.

"The message shall also contain a warning," said Mirkovitch grimly.

"That in case the police are mixed up in the matter —- ?"

"They would not even find a dead body."

A pause followed this ominous speech. This was the dark side of this daring plot: the possible murder of a helpless prisoner. Yet they all knew it might become inevitable; the hostage's life might have to be weighed against theirs in case of discovery, and, instead of barter, there might be need for revenge.

"They will never dare refuse," said the president, endeavouring to dispel the gloom cast over most of these young people by the suggestion of a cold-blooded murder; "there will be no need for measures so unworthy of us."

"They know completely the Tsarevitch's life is in our hands," said Mirkovitch authoritatively. "They cannot defy us, they are bound to treat and bargain with us. We might demand the freedom of every convict now languishing in Siberia, and they would have to remember that the heir of all the Russias sleeps with a dagger held over his heart, and be bound to grant what we ask."

"But let them be just and merciful, and we will be so likewise," added the president's more gentle voice; "let Dunajewski and all those concerned cross the frontier with a free pass, and that day the Tsarevitch will be restored to liberty. But let Alexander understand that at the slightest suspicion of police intervention, the life of the hostage will from that hour be considered forfeited."

There was no reply to this; the president has been putting into words the decision of all those assembled.

Mirkovitch still sat, his powerful fist clutched on the table, in his eyes a dark, lurid fire that told of dangerous thoughts.

"There is one person whom, I think, the committee have omitted to consider," said a voice at last, breaking the silence, that had lasted some minutes, "and that is Lavrovski."

"Pardon me," said the president, "we have, I think, all thought of that incompetent, though, at the present moment, important personage, and all reflected as to what his possible attitude would be throughout."

"I have not the slightest doubt," said a voice from the further end of the table, "that it will take Lavrovski some days before he will make up his mind to communicate with his own government."

"Yes," assented another, "I have met him in Petersburg once or twice, and he always given me the idea being a weak and irresolute man."

"Whose first feeling, when he realises-and it will take him some days to do that-that the Tsarevitch has effectually disappeared, will be one of intense terror, lest the blame for the disappearance be primarily laid on him, and he be dispatched to Siberia to expiate his negligence."

"And the fool puts up with being treated a mere valet to a dynasty who would treat him with such baseness and serving a government which, at the first opportunity, would turn on him and whip him like a cur," muttered Mirkovitch wrathfully.

"We have, therefore, every chance that in our favour," resumed the president, "that Lavrovski will *not* communicate with Petersburg, at any rate for the first few days, whilst he will be busying himself in trying to obtain some clue or idea as to his charge's whereabouts."

"He may probably," suggested someone, "employ some private detective in this city, and, until that hope has failed him, endeavour to keep the Tsarevitch's disappearance a secret from the Russian government."

"Be that as it may," concluded the president. "I think we may safely presume that our messenger will get a few day's start on that slowly moving courtier, and that three days is all he will need to seek out Taranïew, who will lose no time in seeing that the letter reaches its proper destination."

"You are, of course, presuming all the time," now said a voice-an elderly man's voice, sober and sedate-"that Lavrovski, thinking only of his own safety, will at first merely endeavour to keep the matter of the disappearance of his charge's much of a secret as possible; those of our friends who know him best, seem, by judging his pretty well known dilatoriness, to have arrived at this conclusion, which no doubt is the right one. But we must all remember that there is one other person-shall I say enemy?-whom Lavrovski may, in spite of his fears, choose for a confidant, and that person is neither dilatory nor timorous, and has moreover an army of allies of every rank in Vienna to help her speedily and secretly-you all know who I mean."

The question was not answered. What need was there of it? They all knew her by reputation-the beautiful Madame Demidoff-and all suspected and feared her; yet who dared to say she was a spy or worse, this *grande dame* who was one of the ornaments of Viennese society.

"I spoke to her at the opera ball to-night," said Iván Volenski, who up to this point had taken very little part in the discussion.

"She was there then?" queried an anxious voice.

"She always is everywhere where there is a brilliant function," replied Iván, "and it is just possible that she may have had instructions to keep her dainty ears open, whenever she came across any of her compatriots; when I met her, it was just after Maria Stefanowa had driven off in the *fiaker*, Madame Demidoff was wanting her carriage, and asked me to help her in finding it."

"No doubt she is our greatest danger," said the president, "for if anything did rouse her suspicions to-night, she certainly would not hesitate to employ a whole army of private and police detectives, and may force our hand before our brothers in Petersburg have had time to play the trump card."

"After all," said Mirkovitch, "if we find that she is exerting her powers too much, it is always within our means to give her a warning, that the Tsarevitch's life is in actual danger through her interference."

"Anyhow, my friends," now concluded the president, "it is well that, knowing our foes, we keep a strict watch on them. After all, let us always remember that, though we risk our lives and liberties, they, in their turn, must first see that the Tsarevitch is quite safe. We hold the most precious of hostages; for once we are absolute masters of the situation. I don't think we gain anything by discussing any further what Lavrovski and Madame Demidoff may or may not do. They must be strictly watched, that is evident, but the message to Taranïew is the most important; we can include as many conditions in our letter as we like, and leave them at Petersburg to do the rest."

"Yes, the message, the papers," was the unanimous assent to the president's last decision.

He took up the papers one by one that were lying on the table, and divided them into two bundles.

"These," he said, handing one of the packets to his neighbour, "are not of much value, and in view of the approaching crisis, in my opinion had better be destroyed. Will you glance through them and decide?"

The papers were handed round, carefully examined by most of the present and the president's decision being endorsed, they were consigned to the flames.

"This," said the president, with a certain amount of solemnity, "is our account of the Tsarevitch's abduction, as planned and executed by us; and this is the letter, which Taranïew must find means of conveying into Alexander III's own hands; these two papers, together with this small bundle of notes and plans, relating to our brotherhood, are the vital things that we will entrust to our messenger for safe delivery into Taranïew's keeping. We are thus not giving into his hands, not only our own lives and liberty, who are assembled here to-night, but the last hopes of Dunajewski and our unfortunate companions who are in prison. Would to God there were no such necessity for so much written matter-hopelessly compromising so many of us-to be taken across the frontier, but unfortunately that necessity is an imperative one, and we must remember that we all may trust our messenger implicitly."

All eyes now turned towards Iván Volenski, as, almost trembling with emotion, he had received, from the president's hands, the letters and papers which were held out towards him.

Descended from an ancient and once glorious family, Iván Volenski was now the private secretary and confidant to his Eminence Cardinal d'Orsay, the Papal Nuncio, accredited to the courts of Paris, Vienna and Petersburg. But the Polish blood within him could not rest peacefully in the midst of comfortable surroundings. The spirit of plotting peculiar to his countrymen-fanatical, hot-headed and enthusiastic-had thrown him into the arms of this Socialistic brotherhood, for whose sake he daily risked his position, his liberty, his very life.

In the midst as it were of diplomatic and social life, Iván Volenski was a priceless ally to these plotters, who needed men of his stamp, that mixed in with the very society they wished to annihilate, and could keep them well informed of the comings and goings of the exalted personages whom that wished to attack.

It was Volenski who found out for his comrades that the Tsarevitch was in Vienna under the strictest incognito, attended only by an elderly court functionary, and a confidential Russian valet, and staying at the Hotel Imperial under an assumed name, and in the guise of a private gentleman, remaining in town to view the Carnival.

Then is was that the daring plan was conceived by some of these fanatics, to obtain possession of so august a hostage, and then barter his liberty against that of some comrades in Russia, who, implicated an abortive intrigue, were awaiting condemnation, languishing in a Moscow prison.

Iván Volenski now leaned across the table and said, turning towards the president:

"I am happy and proud to feel that it is my power to render the brotherhood so great a service. I will convey the letter, the news, and the papers, safely to Petersburg."

Many hands were stretched across the table towards the young Pole, who grasped them warmly.

"When can you start?" asked Mirkovitch.

"In about two days," replied Iván.

"Too late; cannot you go before?"

"Impossible! The Nuncio leaves Vienna the day after to-morrow. I shall be forced to remain twenty-four hours longer to finish and classify his correspondence, after that I am free and can start immediately."

"Let Iván act as he thinks best," said the president; "not one of us could cross the fr0ontier as safely as he, and a delay of three days is so dangerous as the entrusting of the papers to anyone else."

"So far I have never been suspected," said Volenski reassuringly; "true, those brutes on the frontier did seize and search all my papers once," he added sullenly; "that was after Dunajewski's arrest, when every Pole was an object of that type of tyranny. Fortunately I was not carrying anything compromising then."

"And this time?" asked an anxious voice.

"I shall take the precaution of wrapping our papers in an envelope which I shall stamp with the seal of the Papal Legation. My position is well known, and the papers will be safe enough."

"Fairly safe, shall we say?" retorted a grim voice from the further end of the room.

"Anyhow, it is obvious that we can have no safer messenger then Iván," decided the president; "his is the only plan that promises the slightest measure of safety."

A general murmur of approval confirmed his decision.

"In four days, then, from now, I pledge to you my word that these papers will be handed over by me to Taranïew and the Petersburg committee," said the young Pole with fervour, "together with the news of the glorious act we have accomplished to-night, which is to result in the freedom of Dunajewski and our other comrades, whom we had looked on as lost. And will you tell me now, as my duties with his Eminence may prevent my seeing you before I start, what you propose to do in the meanwhile?"

"There is very little we can do," said the president; "some of us will watch Lavrovski; others, Madame Demidoff. If there is the slightest suspicion of them moving in the matter and calling in police aid, we will convey to them the same warning that Taranïew will submit at headquarters."

"Remember, Volenski," added another member of the committee, "that our anxiety for the safety of our papers and of you, our messenger, will have reached its culmination point on the fourth day from this; and that if you can do so with prudence, try to communicate with us as soon as you have seen Taranïew."

"I will certainly do so," said Iván. "Never fear, the papers will be quite safe; as soon as I have delivered them I shall find my way towards the frontier, where I shall await Dunajewski and our comrades with the money, the committee has entrusted me with, for them. They will be in need of that, moreover, I shall be very happy to shake hands with them and tell them-for they shall be ignorant of it-how we effected there release."

The discussion was closed now; cigarettes and pipes appeared once more, and with a quiet hum of conversation, where no mention of plot or Tsar was made, took the place of enthusiastic discussion. The president was chatting quietly with Volenski, who had slipped the precious papers into his breast-pocket.

Iván was the first to rise.

"I must leave you all now," he said. "When we meet again it will be on my return from Petersburg, when our great work is all complete, and Dunajewski with our comrades are free once more to join us in studying how best to accomplish the weal of Russia and of her people. Good night, all."

"Good night!"

"God-speed!"

A score of hands were stretched out towards him, their friend, their comrade. In the minds of some of them, perhaps, there rose the thought that they might never see their daring messenger again; but these, who had these thoughts, were the older men-those who knew that no scrap of paper is ever really safe in Russia. Inwardly they called forth a blessing, and perhaps a prayer for his safety, as he shook hands with all his friends.

They were all preparing to depart, as they obviously could discuss nothing further that evening, and most of them, though Socialist at heart, were also young besides, and longed to take a last glance at the merrily lighted streets of the city, the gay festivities of the Carnival.

And ten minutes later these men who had so daringly organised, so successfully carried through, one of the most audacious plots in the annals of secret societies, were mixing gaily with the mad throng, bandying jests with merry masks, and seemingly forgetting that there were such things as princely hostages and secret missions, or that one of their comrades, their chosen messenger, would soon-holding all of their lives in his hands-have to convey their secrets to Petersburg, in the very teeth of the most astute police in the world.

Chapter IV

IVÁN VOLENSKI has spoken gaily, reassuringly to them all. But what did he know of his own chances of safety across the Russian frontier? Practically nothing.

Suspect? Bah! Anybody might at the moment become "suspect" to the Russian police. And then, ... that anybody's name is placed on the list.... After that let him try to get across with papers, valuables, secrets, and he will soon find what it means to be a "suspect."

What did Volenski know of how he stood in the eyes of the Russian police? Living mostly abroad and consorting in a great measure with his own exiled countrymen, some small degree of suspicion was bound to remain attached to his name.

He was a Pole, and, being a Pole, he conspired, not because he believed in all the Utopian theories set forth by his brother conspirators, but because it was in his blood to plot and plan against the existing government.

Whether these plots and plans ever resulted in anything tangible, any great reform out there in Russia, he never troubled his mind much to think. He was too young to think of the future; the present was the only important factor in his existence.

He usually shrank from extreme measures. Mirkovitch's bloodthirsty speeches grated upon his nerves, and having spent a miracle of ingenuity in combining some deadly plot that would annihilate the tyrant and his brood, Iván would have preferred that it should not be carried out at all, but left as a record of what a Pole's mind can devise against his hated conquerors.

It was not indecision; it was horror of a refined and even plucky nature, of deeds that would not brook the light of day. He would have liked to lead a Polish insurrection, but feared to handle an assassin's dagger.

He had vague theories about the "People," lofty notions of their immense brain power, downtrodden by powerful officialism, and he looked forward to the days when that somewhat undefinable quality would frame its own laws, appoint its own rulers. How that great object was to be accomplished he had no practical notions; Mirkovitch said, by killing those in power; Lobkowitz, their much decorated president, said, by careful diplomacy and an occasional wholesome fright. The younger men dreamed, and the older ones plotted, and still the throne of the Romanoffs was far from tottering.

And Iván dreamed with the dreamers and plotted with the plotters, eager to help, yet shrinking from decisive action.

He had discovered the Tsarevitch's proposed incognito journey to Vienna and the opera ball. He was a young man of fashion in society, invaluable to the Socialists, for he went everywhere, heard all the gossip, and repeated to them what they wished to hear.

He planned out the abduction in all its details. Mirkovitch was to lend his house, in which to receive the captive, and his daughter was to entice him therein. Baloukine and his brother were to watch the proceedings. After that, he, Iván, would do something perilous, all alone, he cared not what, as long as he did not have to lend a hand in abducting a helpless youth into a dangerous trap.

Nicholas Alexandrovitch had fallen into that trap, with his eyes shut, wholly unsuspecting. It had been well set at the time and place where most young men, be they prince or peasant, are eager for adventures, and the Tsarevitch was barely twenty, and had come the Vienna to enjoy himself.

The bright eyes of the odalisque, as seen through her black velvet mask; seemed full of promise of enjoyment to come; her manners essentially Viennese, were provoking to the verge of distraction, and human nature, ever disguised in the garb of the heir to an empire, would have to undergo very radical changes, ere at twenty years of age it could resist the blandishments of so enterprising an odalisque.

He had jumped into the *fiaker* after her, only thinking of those bright eyes and provoking ways, and the short journey between the opera house and Huemarkt only ended in more complete turning that young head, and subjugating the inflammable heart; for, during those five minutes, Nicholas had succeeded in dislodging the black velvet mask, and in ascertaining that the charms that it held hidden were equally enchanting as those it had revealed. Perhaps had been less young, and therefore more observant, he would not have failed to notice that a slightly sarcastic hovered round the dainty, childlike mouth and a look-was it of pity?–gave those bright eyes an added charm.

The *fiaker* had stopped under a portico, that would have seemed dreary and desolate, beyond description, to the most casual observer, but Nicholas Alexandrovitch flew up the great, dark, stone staircase with no thought save for the dainty figure that ran swiftly up some few *mètres* in front of him. He followed her through a massive door, behind which he had seen her disappear, and found himself in a brilliantly-lighted, dome-like hall, where a well-laden supper-table oc-cupied the centre, looking most tempting, whilst a valet, in irreproachable attitude, mute and expectant, stood by.

As the heavy door fell to behind him, with a loud and reverberating crash, Nicholas Alexan-drovitch, looking around him, realised that the fair odalisque had once more disappeared.

A door at the opposite end of the hall was open; Nicholas passed through it, to find himself in a comfortably furnished bedroom, obviously arranged for a bachelor's wants. It seemed to have no other egress but the door at which the Tsarevitch stood still, amazed, wondering where that bewitching houri had given him the slip. Somewhere on that dark, stone staircase no doubt, and Nicholas pondered as to whether he should endeavour to follow her in that game of hide-and-seek which she appeared to have at her fingers' ends, or calmly await her return, which could, obviously, not be long delayed.

The valet still stood, correct in attitude and dress, mute and expectant. His intense impas-siveness grated on the young prince's turbulent nerves, strung to aching point whilst waiting for the odalisque who did not reappear.

Then it began to strike him as strange, that though the supper appeared sumptuous and plentiful, it had only been laid for one; for the unknown odalisque no doubt; but then, the bedroom adjoining was obviously not a lady's room. Nicholas frowned, and forced his nerves to be still, and his brains to recommence to act; a breath of suspicion-the first-seemed to have crossed his mind. He walked deliberately to the door-it was locked. It did not surprise him, the breath of suspicion had suddenly developed into a hurricane of doubt.

"Where am I?" he asked the valet.

The latter bowed very humbly and pointed to his own ears and mouth, shaking his head the while.

"Real or assumed?" was the Tsarevitch's mental query.

Obviously it was no use to try and force that door, it looked solid enough to resist an assault. Nicholas understood that he had been trapped, for what purpose remained yet to be proven.

A few moments elapsed, then the door was gently open from without; the deaf-mute valet went up towards it. The thought of making a rush for that same door may have presented itself to Nicholas' mind then, but fortunately the humiliation of an unsuccessful attempt was spared him, for behind the door stood two stalwart *moujiks*, equally mute as their comrade, and equally correct in bearing; one of them stepped forward, and with deep obeisance presented a letter to the Tsarevitch, who tore it open impatiently.

A few words only, to tell him what he already knew, that he was a helpless prisoner without hope of escape. His life inviolate, but held as hostage, pending negotiations with his exalted father, which no doubt would soon terminate in a most satisfactory way. And in the meanwhile the lodgings, poor as they were, were entirely at the august prisoner's disposal, as well as three deaf-mute *moujiks* told off to do his bidding.

Nicholas Alexandrovitch called himself a fool, then tried to become a philosopher. He had every confidence in the far-seeing, far-reaching police of his country, trusted to Lavrovski to use every effort and every dispatch, and resigned himself to the inevitable with the character placidity of his race. One last tribute to youth and folly he paid, when he felt an aching pang at the thought that the provoking odalisque had only used her blandishments for purposes so far removed from his poetic imagination. The next half-hour saw the heir of the Tsar of all the Russias eating a sumptuous supper all alone-and a prisoner-with a youthful appetite, and no thoughts for the morrow.

As for Count Lavrovski, in attendance upon his Imperial Highness, he, no doubt, was in a worst position then his abducted charge.

To have allowed the Tsarevitch, for whom he was, so to speak, responsible, to so completely slip through his fingers, was an event unparalleled in the history of a Russian courtier. No doubt, the case being unprecedented, the punishment would be equally so, and Lavrovski already, half an hour after the Tsarevitch's disappearance, could, when shutting his eyes, see visions of convicts, of prisons, of mines, and Siberia.

Half an hour is a long time for the son of the Tsar to remain unattended, and when two or three hours had slipped by, and the crowds of mummers had begun to thin, Lavrovski began to enduring mental tortures he had up to that time had no conception of. And when presently, at some small hour of the morning, the last of the giddy throng were preparing to depart, the old Russian still sat staring into the crowd, cramped in body, and with mental faculties rendered numb with nameless terrors.

The officials asked him to leave; the lights were being turned out, and Lavrovski had perforce to leave his box and find his way into the streets. One or two discreet questions to porters and attendants about an odalisque and a domino brought only mirth for an answer. Fifty odalisques, two thousand dominoes, had passed up and down the opera-house steps during the last few hours.

At the Hotel Imperial, the sleepy hall porter had not seen the young stranger, and the Russian valet, the only attendant to the young Tsarevitch, made a mute inquiry as to his master, which he dared not put into words.

The man would have to be told something; he was trustworthy-might be of help. Lavrovski told him half a truth.

The Tsarevitch had thought fit to go on a young man's escapade. They two must keep that a secret; Nicholas Alexandrovitch might return to-morrow, he might be away some days.

Count Lavrovski could not say; he relied on Stepán to be discreet.

The next day, when no news came, the old Russian began to look longingly at a tiny revolver, he always carried with him. Better that, than to be dragged home to Russia, arraigned for high treason, and sent to Irkutsk to dig salt for the Imperial Exchequer, for having neglected his duties as keeper and caretaker of the young heir to the throne.

But Lavrovski was over sixty, and at that age life seems very sweet, a dear friend we have known for so long, and therefore from whom we are loth to part. He replaced the pistol in his dressing-bag, and looked elsewhere for counsel and guidance.

A good detective-private, not official-might save matter sand unearth the truant, if he was still alive. Well! if he were not, Lavrovski life was in any case not worth an hour's purchase, and the revolver would always be handy.

Stepán asked no questions. Lavrovski looked harassed and anxious; and that was sufficient information for the stolid Russian.

The morning papers had no account of mysterious dead bodies found looted in the streets, and Lavrovski sallied forth to seek a detective.

They recommended him one at one of the news paper offices-M. Furet, a Frenchman, a man of wide experience and good connection.

Lavrovski went to him. He had tried so far not to think too much; the thoughts to which he did not allow coherence, would have led him to a lunatic asylum, and he wished to keep his mind clear of all things, save his duty to his missing charge and to the honour of his own name.

M. Furet was astute, wise, but not omnipotent. Lavrovski told him too little; he felt it as he spoke. The detective, a Frenchman, guessed there was some mystery, and tried to probe the Russian's secret.

But Lavrovski was obdurate. When the time came for throwing himself on the detective's discretion he shrank for the task, dared not avow to him the identity of the missing stranger, and only spoke vaguely of him as a young foreigner of distinction.

The matter was hopeless. M. Furet was waxing inpatient.

"Monsieur," he said at last, "it seems to me that you have come here to-day with the idea no doubt of enlisting my services in a cause which you have at heart, but also with the firm determination to keep your secrets to yourself. You will, I am sure, on thinking the matter over, see how impossible you have made it for me to be of much service to you."

"Can you do nothing then?" asked Lavrovski in despair.

He seemed so dejected, so broken-hearted, that the detective glanced up at him with a certain amount of pity, and said:

"Will you go home, monsieur, and give the matter your full consideration, quietly and deliberately? Read the police news carefully to ascertain that no mysterious death had occurred, or unknown dead body found. I, in the meanwhile, will make what exhaustive enquiries I can, both at the opera house, the *fiaker* stations, and at the different railways. Your truant may, after all, reappear in the next day or two. Young men are often led into adventures, that last longer then two or three days. Then come back and see me on a Saturday afternoon, but come back armed with the determination to tell me *all.* If you cannot bring yourself to do that, do not come at all, and in that case, if I, in the meanwhile, have not found the slightest clue, I will consider the matter dropped as far as I am concerned. And now will monsieur excuse me; my time is valuable, and I have many clients to see."

M. Furet rose; the interview was over. Lavrovski felt there was nothing more to be done unless he fully made up his mind whether he could confide in a third person or not, and that, for the present, he was not prepared to do. The Frenchman might after all be speaking truly; there was every chance that the Tsarevitch was but perusing a young man's adventure, and nothing further could be lost by waiting. If those who had abducted him had meant any harm to him, the harm would by now be accomplished, and the three days Lavrovski gave himself as a respite-either for the return of the prodigal, if he was alive and unharmed, or for throwing himself on the Tsar's doubtful mercy, if evil had come to Nicholas Alexandrovitch-could matter little.

He took up his hat, and promising M. Furet to think he case over, in the light he had suggested, bowed to the old detective, and soon found himself in the streets once more.

He had determined to wait till Saturday, therefore wait he would, without confiding in anyone, still trusting that this terrible adventure would end happily before then, and in the meanwhile bearing his own burden of anxiety alone.

The only person that would of necessity require some sort of explanation - humble in position though he was-was Nicholas' valet. However little intelligence the man might possess, it would yet strike him as suspicious that his master should leave the hotel, and stay with friends so unexpectedly, that he did not even arrange for the most ordinary necessities of his toilet to be brought to him. Lavrovski, therefore, determined to tell him the partial truth-the truth, that is to say, such as he himself would wish it to be.

"You must understand, Stepán," he explained, "that his Imperial Highness has thought it fit to absent himself from this hotel for two or three days. But before leaving he gave me the strictest injunctions that we are to keep his absence the most profound secret form everybody, both here and at home. It is not for you, or even I, to question the Tsarevitch's right to do as he pleases; all we can do is to obey his orders as accurately as we can. To everyone, therefore, his Imperial Highness is confined to his bed with an attack of German measles, which is not serious but might last some days. Now do you quite understand me? and can his Imperial Highness entirely rely upon you fidelity and discretion, both now and in the future?"

"Nicholas Alexandrovitch is my master," said the Russian simply; "he has always found me faithful when he wanted my help, silent when he required my silence. The words I speak are as much at his commands as the deeds I do; I will say what he wishes, or hold my tongue as he desires."

"That is well, Stepán," said Count Lavrovski; "be sure his Imperial Highness will remember what you do for him to-day."

Lavrovski knew he could rely on this man; all was well then for the next two days. After that-in God's hands, he thought, with characteristic Oriental fatalism.

Chapter V

"AND must your Eminence really leave us tomorrow?" said the Emperor Franz Jozef I., with polite regret, as Cardinal d'Orsay, Papal Nuncio accredited to the court of Vienna, prepared to rise for the final leave-taking.

"Indeed, your majesty, did not most imperative duty call me away, I would never of my own accord have left this charming and hospitable city. As it is —— " The Cardinal sighed, and a resigned expression crossed the aristocratic features of this martyr to his duty.

"I am glad, indeed, to think your Eminence has found Vienna so attractive."

"Not so much Vienna, your Majesty, though the city is delightful in itself, but the Viennese — - !" The Cardinal paused, for once in his diplomatic career, words failed him with which to convey his thoughts of this interesting subject.

"You will find in the *grandes dames* of St. Petersburg formidable rivals to those of Vienna," said the Emperor pensively.

his Eminence did not reply. He recollected one or two little perfumed breaths of scandal that had reached his ears, of how one of those *grandes dames* of St. Petersburg had, last winter, found in Franz Jozef's large and inflammable heart an undisputed if somewhat temporary place. There was silence for a few moments. The Emperor was evidently ill at ease, his hand was toying nervously with the trifling knick-knacks that adorned his writing-table, whilst once or twice he seemed as if about to speak, then checked himself abruptly.

The Cardinal, whose long diplomatic career had taught him the science of quiet patience, leant back in his chair and waited for what, he knew, the Emperor still wished to say to him.

"Your Eminence will be seeing many of my old friends at St. Petersburg," said the Emperor at last, with evasive irrelevance.

"I will make a point of seeing *all* those your Majesty would wish me to see," replied the Cardinal with pointed courtesy.

"Your Eminence is most kind, and I feel sure will convey my friendly greetings to the Tsar and Tsaritsa in a far worthier manner than my poor pen could express. I would also wish to be kept in the *bons souvenirs* of the Grand Duchess Xenia and the Grand Duke, of whose last visit to Vienna I have such agreeable recollections."

The Cardinal smiled imperceptibly, and his eyes rested for an infinitesimal space of time on a dainty miniature, set in old paste, which no doubt portrayed one of those agreeable recollections.

Swift as had been the Cardinal's glance, Franz Jozef evidently had caught it, for he added somewhat nervously:

"And do not forget to lay my humble respects at the feet of the Princess Marïonoff, who, I trust, will soon visit Vienna again, the scene of her last carnival's triumphs."

"Any written or verbal message your Majesty deigns to entrust me with will be safely delivered," once more assented Cardinal d'Orsay.

"Take care," said the Emperor, with a nervous laugh, "I may take your Eminence at your word, and send such voluminous messages as will encumber your overladen trunk."

"My services are at your Majesty's command."

The Emperor looked keenly for a moment or two longer at his Eminence's astute, diplomatic face, then, as if obeying a sudden impulse, he took a small key from his pocket and, opening one of the larger drawers of his writing-table, he carefully pulled out a voluminous parcel and placed it before Cardinal d'Orsay's astonished gaze.

"And if I were to ask your Eminence to let my message take this form?" said Franz Jozef at last.

Throughout his career his Eminence had never once been taken wholly by surprise, but this time, just for the space of a second, his deep-set eyes seemed to open a trifle wider than usual with astonishment.

"The message, in fact, is a souvenir," continued the Emperor, "a mere trifle, that will make the recipient remember Vienna and the Viennese, in a way I would wish her to do."

"Her?"

"Yes!"

"Ah! I understand. The Grand Duchess Xenia," said his Eminence, with a thought of malice.

"No! not the Grand Duchess; she would not value works of art such as these."

"They are works of art?"

"Of the rarest kind, anad intended for a connoisseur who will know how to appreciate them."

"Will your Majesty deign to name that connoisseur?"

"The Princess Marïonoff."

"Oh!"

"She has often admired these *bibelots*, and it is not always in our power to completely gratify a beautiful woman's whim. I am anxious to show your Eminence the humble gift that I will ask you to lay at the Princess' feet."

With infinite care and patience the Emperor, with his own hands, proceeded to unfold the parcel from its numerous papers and wrappings, and presently displayed before his Eminence's admiring gaze a pair of the most dainty, most valuable china candlesticks that ever adorned a marquise's boudoir.

Each candlestick represented a Cupid, in that rarest of all wares known as *vieux Vienne*, with arms outstretched, shooting a golden arrow from a gigantic bow at an imaginary target. The feet were firmly planted upon a basis of exquistely chased gold, the figure slightly leaning against the trunk of a tree, which was pure gold, and the branches of which formed the receptacle for the candles.

"Truly a charming, an appropriate gift," said the Cardinal in admiration, though with a touch of sarcasm.

Ever since he had realised the nature of the message the Emperor wished to convey to his *chère amie*, his Eminence had seemed decidedly less eager to place his services at Franz Jozef's disposal. The candlesticks seemed so fragile, and yet would be so cumbersome, that Cardinal d'Orsay almost shuddered at the grave responsibility of taking about so much brittle ware with him, across some two thousand miles of country.

But the Emperor appeared wholly unconscious of the Cardinal's lack of enthusiasm. With the eagerness of a connoisseur he pointed out the exquisite modelling of the china, and the dainty chasing of the gold.

"And to add to the charm and rarity of the *bibelots*," he added, "these candlesticks contain a thought of mystery. Will your Eminence press very lightly on this small leaf that stands apart from the rest on this little gold twig?"

The Cardinal obeyed good-humouredly, and, to his astonishment, saw that the leaf concealed a tiny spring, which, when touched, displayed a hidden receptacle, velvet lined, in the hollow of the tree-trunk.

"This secret spring is the most interesting feature of these candlesticks," explained the Emperor; "my great-aunt, the unfortunate Marie Antoinette, succeeded in sending a most important message to her brother through the medium of these innocent-looking *bibelots* and the help of M. de Neuperg."

The Cardinal had often heard the story of the secret means M. de Neuperg found, of taking the unhappy queen's messages safely across the French frontier. Surely these candlesticks, then, were an heirloom, almost a relic; they had-he had heard-stood in the Hofburg chapel since the unforunate queen's death, until the day when a pair of beautiful Russian eyes had looked at them longingly; and now the treasures were gaily passing out of the martyr's family for ever.

The Cardinal was silent; he would have given a good deal had he found some remotely plausible excuse for not executing the Emperor's commission. He foresaw all kinds of eventualities, resulting in fractures to the dainty china limbs or even to the gold branches and leaves, and saw terrible visions of arriving at St. Petersburg with half a Cupid and a leafless trunk.

"I need not add, I feel sure," said his Majesty, breaking a silence that threatened to become awkward, "that I entirely rely on your Eminence's discretion in the matter. You see, both the Queen Regent of Spain and the Comtesse de Paris have perhaps a right in thinking that these candlesticks should not pass out of my hands into any but theirs; and I would prefer that my subjects should know nothing of this delicate mission, which I beg of your Eminence to accept for me."

"Your Majesty may quite rely upon me; my discretion has, I think, been often tried, and never been found wanting."

There was a want of cordiality about his Eminence's manner now, but the Emperor was too intent on once more packing up his treasures to notice a trifling detail of that sort. He had secured an emissary-the most discreet in Europe-for the conveying of his gift, and he was determined not to give him a chance of taking back his half-given word.

The candlesticks were once more safely packed up, and the Emperor seemed eager not to prolong the interview, now that he had his wish and Cardinal d'Orsay's final promise.

"I shall never cease to be grateful to your Eminence for this friendly service," he said finally, and stretched out a cordial hand towards the Cardinal with that happy mixture of dignity and *bonhomie* that is the characteristic feature of the Hapsburgs, and that no one yet has been able to resist.

The Cardinal bowed low over the Imperial hand, and, though his face wore the resigned expression of a martyr to duty, he contrived to take a final farewell of Franz Jozef that left a cheering impression on that much-harassed monarch's mind.

A few minutes later Cardinal d'Orsay was in his carriage on his way home, a voluminous parcel on the seat in front of him, and a look of suppressed annoyance on his usually impassive face.

Chapter VI

Iᴛ had already been settled, some little time ago, that his Eminence Cardinal d'Orsay would leave Vienna on the day following-Thursday-to take two or three weeks' relaxation from his diplomatic duties, under the strictest incognito, somewhere among the mountains of Bohemia.

He had terminated his mission from his Holiness Leo XIII to his Catholic and Apostolic Majesty Franz Jozef I with that ease and tact which characterised all his Eminence's methods of procedure, whether diplomatic or otherwise, and would presently be going to St. Petersburg also on a diplomatic mission, but one of a most intricate character, which would require all his Eminence's skill and knowledge of the world and of that Imperial enigma-the Tsar.

Iván Volenski had been kept incessantly at work all that day, ever since his Eminence had returned from Low Mass, classifying and arranging the diplomatic correspondence relating to the concluded mission, and preparing the documents that the Nuncio would require when, having returned from his well-earned holiday, he would be ready to start for St. Petersburg.

Iván had worked hard, chiefly to calm his agitation and force his mind to wander away from visions of various possible occurences on the dreaded Russian frontier, which had haunted him during the night. Also he was anxious to conclude all his duties connected with the Legation; he was eager to start as soon as possible, to hand over the terrible responsibility of the papers, which already was weighing him down heavily.

It was late in the afternoon when his Eminence returned from his final leave-taking of his Majesty. Iván, who was waiting for him, noticed at once the look of annoyance that seemed to ruffle the Cardinal's placid features.

"Cardinal proposes and Emperor disposes!" said his Eminence wearily, after he had with the greatest care deposited his precious burden on the table. "Iván, my son, I have bad news to tell you."

"Bad news, your Eminence?"

"Don't look so scared, my son; it is merely a matter of a great inconvenience and of a bitter disappointment. I shall not be able to go to Carlsbad to-morrow."

"Oh?"

"No; I am to be Cupid's messenger instead. Truly a novel form of diplomacy, even after my years of experience. And this," added his Eminence, pointing to the bulky parcel on the table, "is the message I am to take."

"But I do not understand. Where is the message to go to?" asked Volenski, somewhat amused at the clerical diplomat's ruffled composure.

"All the way to St. Petersburg, my son, to be laid at the most beautiful feet in the world-those of the Princess Marïonoff-on behalf of his Catholic and Apostolic Majesty Franz Jozef I."

"And your Eminence has undertaken to convey this unwieldy parcel all the way to St. Petersburg, and are giving up your holiday in order to satisfy the Emperor's caprice?" asked Volenski in astonishment.

"What could I do?" said the Cardinal impatiently. "You know how insinuating the Hapsburg family can be-its respected chief more so than anyone in the world. His Majesty had extracted a promise from me and forced these things into my hand before I had fully recovered from the astonishment in which his request had plunged me."

"So now your Eminence intends putting off your trip to Carlsbad indefinitely and delivering the Emperor's message, first of all?" asked Iván, who suddenly became nervous as to how these altered plans would affect his own movements.

"Yes! I am anxiouos to get rid of these brittle things-for brittle they are to an alarming degree—I should never know a moment's peace till they were out of my hands, and safe in those of the fair sorceress, who has succeeded in inveigling Franz Jozef into giving her so precious an heirloom. We will start for St. Petersburg to-morrow."

"We?"

"Yes, my son! I am afraid you must, like myself, find your holiday indefinitely postponed. Having once got so far, I shall push on to Peterhof at once, and see his Majesty the Tsar, for whom his Holiness has entrusted me with a memorial, and settle all my work in Russia, with your help, as quickly as possible."

Volenski did not reply. In his mind there arose the fact of the great additional safety to his own secret mission, if he were actually travelling in attendance upon his Eminence. Clearly this change of plans was for the good of the cause.

"I shall be quite ready to start to-morrow," he said at last, with ill-concealed alacrity and an involuntary sigh of relief.

"Well! you take it more philosophically than I do, my son," said the Cardinal sadly.

"After all, your Eminence," said Volenski, with an attempt at consolation, "your holiday and mine are only postponed; in a month's time the spring will be upon us-the weather altogether more propitious for pleasure trips."

"In a month's time, my son," said the Cardinal, whose gloom could not so easily be dispelled, "there will no doubt have cropped up some work, that again will brook no delay. There was no time like the present."

"In the meanwhile," said Iván, "will your Eminence allow me to give the parcel to Antoine that he may pack it in one of the boxes?"

"Gently, my son, gently; ah! you do not know the double annoyance these things are causing me; for not only do they necessitate the postponement of our holiday, but they are of such brittle nature that the conveying of them all the way to Petersburg will be one prolonged anxiety to two bachelors like ourselves."

"Indeed?"

"Yes; cut the string, my son, and look at the *bibelots;* you can feast your eyes on the most charming works of art it has ever been my good fortune to see, truly a fitting gift of an Emperor to a Princess."

Volenski had already opened the parcel, and, with the eyes of a connoisseur, was admiring the exquisite workmanship, the grace of design, of these truly unique *bibelots.*

"Their history," added his Eminence, "as His Majesty told me, is as interesting as the works of art themselves. The candlesticks are not entirely what they seem, and there is a charming secret about them."

"A secret?"

"See," said his Eminence, explaining to Iván the intricacies of the hidden spring, "history has it that Queen Marie Antoinette used these candlesticks as a means of sending private messages to her relatives in Vienna. The secret, apparently, has been well kept, for until now the Hapsburgs never allowed these treasures to stand anywhere but in the Hofburg chapel, and no one, I believe, until this day, has ever seen these mysterious receptacles."

Volenski had turned pale with suppressed excitement; his hand slightly trembled as, with unwonted eagerness, he now once more examined the Emperor's candlesticks. He listened to his Eminence with an earnestness which was not wholly that of a mere connoisseur. A wild, a grand idea had suddenly surged in his brain. Here was safety at last: complete, unassailable. A place wherein to deposit the valuable papers that not the most far-seeing Russian official could dream of; moreover, the candlesticks themselves would be in his Eminence's keeping, and who would dare to touch the belongings of the Papal Nuncio? Now for a little simple diplomacy, and then peace, comfort, freedom from anxiety, till, arrived at St. Petersburg, the papers safely across the frontier, he would have exercised the finest stroke of strategy ever done by any member of the secret society.

"Well, Iván, and what do you think of them?" his Eminence's voice broke in, on Volenski's meditations.

"They are certainly most exquisite works of art," said the young man, pulling himself together, "but I do not wonder that your Eminence is anxious about them; they seem so brittle, so fragile, that one fears damage even in the packing."

"That is why I dare not trust them to Antoine, and had hoped, Iván, that you would see to the packing for me yourself; my own fingers are old and clumsy: it really requires a woman's hand."

"No woman's hands can be more careful than mine shall be," said Iván eagerly; "I will see about these things at once. They will be safest, I think, in your Eminence's own valise, which can then be placed in the *coupé*, and remain under our own eyes the whole length of the journey."

"You certainly will be relieving my anxiety very considerably, my dear son, by taking charge of these candlesticks for me. I can assure you, that no diplomatic burden has ever weighed so heavily on my shoulders as these fragile *bibelots*."

Fate seemed definitely to have placed herself in league with Volenski's project. Being a Pole, he was superstitious, and sought for the mysterious workings of some supernatural agency, in this most ordinary event.

He was brave in danger, with control over his nerves and fears, but this was an eager kind of emotion-that of joy, relief, triumph-and his arms shook, as he carried the precious candlesticks up to his own private room.

He wished to be alone, to think quietly over the matter, not to allow his eagerness to run away with his reason. His comrades' safety was the important fact to bear in mind, and *that* he would undoubtedly be furthering by concealing the papers in the secret receptacle.

He was excited, enthusiastic!

"God's hand," he thought, "protects the cause. He placed this secret within my reach. And now, in two days, Taranïew can have the papers. his Eminence will have charge of them. The Papal Nuncio himself will unwittingly convey them across the frontier."

his Eminence could not be "a suspect," that was clear; if he declared a parcel to contain works of art belonging to himself, not the chief of the Third Section in person would dare to lay hands on the Cardinal's property.

And feverishly he touched the secret spring of one of the candlesticks, and gazed, almost lovingly, into the velvet-lined receptacle within. Once more assuring himself that his door was safely locked, he took, from out of his breast-pocket, the papers entrusted to him yesterday by the committee, slipped them inside the hollow of the tree-trunk, and carefully closed the spring again. He then minutely examined the two candlesticks, and ascertained that the china Cupid, who was now guarding the papers, had a slightly damaged arm, from wrist to elbow, which made it easily recognisable from its twin. He then wrapped them up carefully in many layers of cotton wool, and multitudinous soft papers, and, taking the precious parcel to the Cardinal's room, he locked it up in his Eminence's valise, side by side with the episcopal ring and other insignia of his sacred calling.

"Yes, your Eminence, you shall take our papers to St. Petersburg for us, hidden in the gift of an Emperor to a Princess; they will be safe enough there, I think."

Five minute later Iván, calm once more, sought out the Cardinal in his study; he handed him over the key to his valise, and gave him the assurance that the Emperor's candlesticks were quite safely packed, without fear of the slightest damage.

"I am infinitely grateful to you, my son," said his Eminence; "and now, as I am myself dining out, I think I may safely give you this, your last evening in Vienna, to dispose of, and say good-bye to any friends you may wish to see. You will have to leave instructions about our intended departure by the morning's express, and be ready yourself for the journey. Good night, Iván, and thank you."

Volenski retired with a low bow, glad to think that he was off duty for the rest of the day. He hoped that some time during the evening he would meet one or the other of his comrades, and be able to tell him to communicate with the others that, owing to the most propitious circumstances, he would start for Petersburg twenty-four hours sooner than was anticipated. They might, therefore, rest fully assured that the papers would be safe in Taranïew's hands by the Saturday morning at latest, more especially as he would now be travelling actually with his Eminence the Nuncio, and that, therefore, there was not the slightest fear of his being asked unpleasant questions, or having his papers examined. Those, belonging to the brotherhood, he had placed in a hiding-place that was unparalleled for safety and defied the eyes of the keenest-sighted Russian official in the Empire.

Chapter VII

THAT same night his Eminence, as he had told Iván, was not dining at his hotel: he was spending an evening-the last of a series-in the company of Madame Demidoff, the most charming, the most mysterious, the most dangerous, of those Russian *grandes dames* who haunt the societies of Vienna, Paris, and London, live on apparently boundless means, are received everywhere, admired by the men, envied by the women, and feared by the staff and even the head of the respective Russian embassies.

Why the beautiful Madame Demidoff should be feared by her own compatriots it were difficult for an Englishman or a Frenchman to say; she was always affable, equally so to everyone whom she meet in society, and appeared not to take the slightest interest in matters political; true, there had been a rumour a year ago that at the Austrian frontier one day an over-zealous custom-house official, in inspecting the luggage of Madame Demidoff, who was going across to Russia, is said to have found some papers, wherein the lady gave a curiously minute account of all the sayings and doings of the Tsar's subjects residing in Vienna, including one or two intimate conversations between "Monsieur l'ambassadeur" and Madame his wife, that had actually taken place in their own bedroom; but this never got beyond a rumour, and the fact that "Monsieur l'ambassadeur" was shortly afterwards asked to retire from the diplomatic service may have had nothing to do with that intimate conversation which, after all, he had had with his wife between four walls and one or two doors. Anyhow, his Excellency, the present ambassador, and all his staff, also "Madame l'ambassadrice," are always particularly amiable with Madame Demidoff, and ask her to all their most select parties-but, the moment she leaves they sigh a sigh of relief, and when her name is mentioned before his Excellency he invariably says, "Do not name her to me; it gives me a cold shiver down the back."

However, all this was rumour pure and simple; nothing definite had ever been said that might throw suspicion of an ignoble calling on so fair an addition to Viennese smart society, and all uncharitable whispers were invariably suppressed by Madame Demidoff's numerous friends and admirers. Moreover, she entertained so superbly-her little dinners were worthy of an ode by the court poet, and her balls were counted among the great functions of the season.

One of these charming little dinners she proposed giving to-night to one of her most ardent, most valued friends, his Eminence Cardinal d'Orsay, who never shamed his high ecclesiastical office by avoiding any pretty woman that was willing to help him to while away the tediousness of diplomatic negotiations.

But she meant to leave for Petersburg that very evening by the midnight express, for it seemed to her beyond a doubt that some mystery was connected with the Tsarevitch's chase after the odalisque at the opera ball last night; and this mystery, unless more power were placed in her hands, she knew herself incapable of solving.

She had seen nothing of Eugen during the day, and the evening was drawing on rapidly; she had but little hope of learning any very important facts from him. The plot-if plot there were-once successfully carried through, proved how well all plans must have been laid; time and place were in its favour, and the information gleaned by inquiries outside the opera house, where the crowd at the time of the abduction numbered hundreds of thousands, was sure to be of very meagre character.

But at present she was actually ignorant as to whether the Tsarevitch had, after all, returned to the hotel and the whole mystery burst as a soap bubble. Then Lavrovski's attitude would be interesting and important to note.

There was a discreet rap at the door of the boudoir, where she had been waiting for the last half-hour, nervously pacing up and down the room, and at times sitting at her desk and covering sheets of paper with rapid scribbling.

"Ah! it is you, Eugen," she said, as, in answer to her impatient "Come in," the *moujik's* stolid figure appeared at the door. "Well! have you learnt anything? Tell me as briefly as you can all the important points while I make notes; you must be quick, for I can only spare a few minutes."

"According to your Excellency's instructions," began the Russian, "I went at once to the opera house, where the last of the masks were then departing, and the lights were being put out; I had conversations with most of the attendants and some of the commissionaires who had been stationed there, but no one seems to have taken much notice of the odalisque, the black domino, or the *fiaker*. They all, however, recollect an elderly gentleman, also in a black domino, making similar inquiries to mine, who seemed very agitated and disappointed when he could learn nothing."

"Lavrovski, of course! Well?"

"At the hotel this morning, I gathered that the Tsarevitch has up to this moment not reappeared, for Count Lavrovski, whom I followed at about two o'clock this afternoon, went off to the business house of a certain M. Furet, who, as I learnt from his *concierge*, is a very well-known and much-thought-of detective in this city."

"H'm! I wonder what his hopes were in that quarter!" mused Madame Demidoff. "You are sure he did not send a telegram across to Petersburg first?"

"Quite sure, your Excellency; I am coming to that presently. What happened at the interview I, of course, cannot say, but what struck me was, that when Count Lavrovski left M. Furet's office half an hour later, he seemed, if possible, more hopelessly dejected than before. I concluded from that —— "

"Never mind conclusions and surmises, my friend; it is facts we want to get hold of," said Madame Demidoff reflectively. "No doubt Lavrovski did not dare to fully confide in this Furet, and the detective, thereupon, would refuse to spend his time on a wild-goose-chase. What happened after that?"

"There is very little more to tell, Excellency. Count Lavrovski went straight back to the hotel, from whence he has not stirred all day. Stepán, the Russian valet, however, went out about five o'clock. I noticed he carried a piece of paper in his hand. I followed him to a telegraph office, and was fortunate enough to catch a glimpse of the contents, as he handed it across the counter."

"And?"

"It contained only a few words: 'Nicholas confined to his bed; doctors say German measles; not the last serious; will be up in less than a week.–Lavrovski.'"

Madame Demidoff sat still awhile now, reflecting on what she had heard, her brows knit, buried in thought. "To whom was the telegram addressed?" was the last question she asked.

"I could not see, Excellency," answered the man. "I could only get one glance at it, and have told you the words that struck me."

She had taken up a sheet of paper, and was making rapid notes of what she had heard. Little enough it seemed as she read them over, and she was tapping her foot with impatience and impotent energy.

"It seems pretty clear that Lavrovski has made up his mind to wait," she said, "and is trying as best he can to keep ignorant at headquarters of the Tsarevitch's disappearance. This is, no doubt, Furet's advice to him, who wants probably to have all the credit of discovering Nicholas' whereabouts, and the liberal reward that is sure in that case to be his.

"I care nothing for the reward, but this mystery alarms me. Lavrovski! Bah! an incompetent personage at best, now a coward, who thinks more of his own safety than of hte dangers that at this moment surround the Tsarevitch in his unknown prison. Pray to God," she added fervently, "that it remain a prison, and not become a grave."

"Amen!" said Eugen.

"Now, Eugen, that is, I think, all that you have to tell me. Your work, after I have left, will not be very difficult. Follow this man Furet wherever he goes, glean every scrap of information you can; remember, if anyone discovers the Tsarevitch it must be I and you, not they. You understand?"

A rumble of carriage wheels was now distinctly audible under the portico. Madame Demidoff hastily finished what writing she had to do, then locked her desk, and dismissed Eugen, who disappeared, silent and stolid as he had come.

Then it was that the consummate histrionic art, which this fascinating woman had at her fingers' ends, ,showed itself in a way that, to a hidden observer, would have seemed almost weird; in the space of less than a minute, she seemed to have thrown off every vestige of anxiety and agitation. Her face was calm and smiling; the words of welcome to her exalted guest seemed ready to bubble forth; the hand that was cordially stretched forward was neither cold nor trembling.

The lackey had thrown open the door and announced:

"his Eminence the Cardinal Archbishop of Beauvaix, Papal Nuncio."

"Your Eminence does my poor house too much honour," she said, with a gracious smile, while the Cardinal, with the gallantry peculiar to his calling, kissed the tips of the dainty fingers that had been placed between his own.

No wonder her countrymen were afraid of her; no wonder it was a slight shiver she occasioned at times, in those who guessed what lay hidden behind the impassive mask of the Russian *grande dame*, the friend of princes, of kings and cardinals; perhaps it was the terror of the unknown, a vague fear caused by this beautiful, impenetrable, and certainly dangerous sphinx.

As for his Eminence, not being a Russian he had no cause to fear Madame Demidoff, but every reason to admire her, and sharpen his diplomatic wit against hers; as for shivers, they certainly were not cold ones she gave him down the back. He saw in her a most brilliant and agreeable conversationalist, who knew everybody that was worth knowing, had been everywhere that was worth visiting; her taste in matters artistic was unerring, her knowledge of interesting *objets d'art* the most complete on record. She had once written a most interesting pamphlet on the thimbles of Catherine II, another on the spurs of Peter the Great; she professed an ardent enthusiasm for the Roman Catholic Church, and showed an equally genuine one for its high dignitaries. Failing a trip to the Bohemia, his Eminence thought the *recherché* little dinners, *en tête-à-tête* with Madame Demidoff, the most consoling, most exhilarating holiday for his much harassed mind.

"And your Eminence is really leaving us to-morrow?" said the fair Russian with a sigh, when, having adjourned to her dainty boudoir after dinner, she sat lazily reclining in an armchair, a gold-tipped cigarette between her fingers, and a pair of arch black eyes fixed coquettishly on the reserved, impassive face of her *vis-à-vis*.

"It is unkind to speak of it at this early hour, madame, and embitter the last pleasing moments I shall spend in this delightful capital," replied the Cardinal.

"Come, come," she added coquettishly, "I did not know that diplomacy completely precluded truthfulness, even at the shrine of gallantry. If rumour speak correctly, your Eminence is only leaving us for newer, and therefore more enjoyable, scenes."

"Alas! *chère madame*, rumour, which spoke truly at morn, now talks falsely at even. I certainly had intended to go to Carlsbad for a fortnight's relaxation among the beautiful mountains —- "

"Incognito?" she asked mischievously.

"Incognito," he smiled in reply. "But, alas! unforeseen duties have since called me elsewhere."

"Why, that is very sudden," she said; "M. Volenski, whom I met last night, told me that your Eminence had completed your work, and were going on leave of absence for three weeks at least."

"Iván Volenski told you what was quite correct last night, but alas! has ceased to be so to-day," sighed his Eminence, with angry impatience.

"And your Eminence is going —- ?" she asked, with truly feminine curiosity.

He looked at her and smiled; she was bewitchingly pretty, smoking her cigarette with that infinite grace so peculiar to Russian women.

"Elsewhere," he said at last, as if in a vain attempt to check any further questions.

But experienced diplomatist as, no doubt, the Papal Nuncio was, this was a false move, for the word, as used by him, obviously hid a mystery. Madame Demidoff bit her lip; she disliked secrets, until they became her own. his Eminence had, quite unwittingly, aroused her curiosity, and she had decided in her mind, in the space of a few seconds, that the Cardinal should not leave her house to-night before having told her where he was going the next day.

"Elsewhere is a vague word," she said poutingly, "not to say ungallant. Your Eminence has not accustomed me to such brusque answers."

Her annoyance, real or assumed, upset the inflammable cleric even more than her archness.

"Believe me, *chère madame*," he said, full of contrition, "that were the secret mine I would confide it you immediately, and not attempt to fence with words with you, which proceeding, I own, seems shockingly ungallant."

"Ah! then you admit that there is a secret connected with your change of plans?"

"Nay! I never denied that, but the secret is not my own."

"Would it be the first time, then, that your Eminence will have entrusted me with a secret which was not wholly yours?" she asked.

Evidently the shaft told truly, for the Cardinal did not reply. She saw she had gained a point. She was now burning with curiosity, and, womanlike, was more determined than ever to pierce his Eminence's last attempts at mystery.

"I thought," she added, with real reproach in her voice, "that when your Eminence did me the honour to employ my poor services to aid you in some of your delicate diplomatic missions, that we had both agreed to share all political secrets with each other."

"This is not a political secret, *chère madame*," protested the Cardinal.

"Private, then? Ah! take care! my jealousy might prove more serious than my curiosity."

"Not my own, I repeat," hastily corrected the Cardinal.

"Whose, then?" she persisted. "Your Eminence told me that you had seen no one this Ash Wednesday save M. Volenski, and —- "

She paused. In a moment she had guessed, and, more than that, had guessed correctly. his Eminence's conscious look spoke volumes.

"So your Eminence is taking a secret private message from His Majesty to some remote place elsewhere," she said, delighted at her first success. "Ah! now you cannot damp my curiosity any more. You must tell me all about it. For whom is the message?....A lady, of course....The Emperor's newest *chère amie*....I have it!...The Princess Mari͏̈onoff!...Your Eminence is going to Petersburg with a *billet doux* from the Emperor to the beautiful Princess Mari͏̈onoff!"

"*Chère madame!*" still feebly protested the Cardinal.

"Ah, your Eminence deserves that, after your want of confidence in me, I should publish the fact in the Viennese papers to-morrow. What a delightful paragraph it would make: 'A cardinal as Cupid's messenger.' Truly the secret is now mine. Mine by right of conquest. Your Eminence should have trusted a tried friend, and might have guessed that a mystery which baffles Madame Demidoff has yet to be invented, and is none of your or his Majesty's making."

The Cardinal was now truly distressed. His much-boasted-of discretion had received a very severe blow, and he was not at all confident but that this enigmatical woman would not take some unpleasant small revenge, such as she threatened.

"Believe me, *chère madame*," he ventured to say at last, "that nothing but the most solemn promise to his Majesty prevented my telling you from the first all that you wished to know. Madame Demidoff's powers of guessing riddles are too widely known for any poor diplomat like myself to attempt to battle against them. I can but throw myself, conquered as I am, entirely at your mercy."

"I will be generous to your Eminence," she said, once more captivating and coquettish; "now that my whim is gratified, I can afford to be merciful, but on one condition only —- "

"And that is?"

"That you tell me what it is you are taking over to the Princess as a gift from her exalted admirer; it cannot be merely a *billet doux*, for the post would have been almost as safe as your Eminence. Is it some rare and valuable gift? Diamonds? Pearls? or *objets d'art?*"

"It is, indeed, a most rare, not to say unique, gift," said the Cardinal, now completely subjugated and resigned; "so absolutely valuable that no diamonds or pearls could ever have purchased them."

"Ah?"

"Madame, remember I am at your mercy; you will consider this in the light of a State secret."

"Have I ever been known to betray any secrets?" she asked impatiently.

"So long as I have your promise ——"

"No need of a fresh promise; surely your Eminence knows me. Come, you have gone too far now to beat a retreat."

"*Voilà!* It appears that last year the beautiful Princess, in admiring the beauties of the Hofburg, thought fit to cast longing eyes on the celebrated candlesticks of gold and *vieux Vienne* that had belonged to Marie Antoinette."

"Ah, yes, I have heard of them; they are said to be most exquisite works of art, and I believe many a member of the Hapsburg family has longed in vain to possess them."

"Until the said pair of Russian eyes were cast on them with a pleading look, and an Imperial heart was unable to resist," assented the Cardinal.

"And his Majesty?"

"Has asked me to lay these same candlesticks, together with the Imperial and Royal homage, at the dainty feet of his *chère amie.*"

"And your Eminence has accepted the task?"

"With great reluctance, I assure you, *chère madame;* but what would you? His Majesty has the faculty of opening even an old diplomatist's heart, as easily as he does the secret springs of his candlesticks."

"The secret springs?"

"Yes! did you not know the candlesticks contained secret springs, with mysterious receptacles, that, according to history, contained many a time Marie Antoinette's private missives to her brother in Vienna? Oh! they are most interesting heirlooms, most fascinating *bibelots.*"

Madame Demidoff said nothing more; for a while she sat pensively watching the clouds of smoke as they rose form her cigarette, and her eyes wandered from time to time towards the Cardinal, who sat absorbed in reflections, probably of that Bohemian trip he was forced to abandon.

"Ah! how I wish I could see those candlesticks!" said madame at last, with an impatient little sigh.

"Have you never seen them? They are certainly the most exquisite works of art it has ever been my good fortune to see."

"Your Eminence, it is truly cruel to torture the soul of a humble collector, like myself, by telling me of treasures I shall now never behold."

"Would that be so great a hardship?" he asked, smiling.

"Oh! do not laugh; I am simply burning with curiosity; all night I shall dream of *vieux Vienne* candlesticks, of gold mounts, of secret springs. How can I imagine a thing that I know must surpass anything of the kind I have ever seen? It will be a nightmare surely."

"Do not say that, *chère madame;* think of the tortures of remorse I shall have to endure, knowing that my momentary indiscretion, in speaking of these *bibelots,* has caused you a restless night."

"Why not avoid the remorse for yourself and the nightmare for me by gratifying my burning curiosity?"

"With all the pleasure in life," said his Eminence, with alacrity, "if madame will honour me by stepping into my carriage and paying my dreary abode a visit, the candlesticks will but need unpacking--"

"Oh, *mon Dieu!* your Eminence! What you propose would be *très compromettant* for me; think of your servants, of M. Volenski."

"Pardon me, madame!" said his Eminence. "I am an old diplomatist, and I ceased to be compromising to a pretty woman many years ago."

"Diplomatists are always compromising, your Eminence! and I really would not dare venture, for fear I should be punished by being forced to take the veil of a Carmelite. But oh!" she added, with a pretty gesture of entreaty, "will your Eminence allow me to send my confidential maid to M. Volenski and ask him to give her the candlesticks? I assure you, I shall not sleep a wink to-night, and to-morrow look as old as Madame l'ambassadrice, unless your Eminence will satisfy my curiosity."

"Madame, among my numerous sins, which, alas! the Recording Angel but too faithfully marks against me, there has often occurred the sin of giving a lady a sleepless night, but never that of causing her to look a day older than her years. I feel sure such a sin would be beyond forgiveness; so, if you will allow me, I will ring for my carriage and drive to my hotel at once, in order to bring you the objects of your curiosity myself. I doubt if Volenski is at home at this moment; moreover, I have the key of my valise in which I know they are locked."

"Oh, your Eminence is too kind!" said Madame Demidoff, with almost childish delight; "you will gauge the extent of my curiosity by the fact that it has completely annihilated my courtesy, inasmuch as I find it impossible to refuse your kind proposition."

And, as if fearing that the Cardinal might change his mind, she rang the bell, and ordered his Eminence's carriage to be brought round immediately. The Cardinal, very much amused at this old yet ever new trait of feminine curiosity, promised not to tarry a moment, and ten minutes later he took a temporary leave, and the roll of his carriage soon died away in the distance.

Madame Demidoff sat for some moments quite still, unable to move-perhaps from sheer intensity of excitement-till the very last sound of those carriage wheels could be heard no more. A torpor, akin to a trance, seemed to have mastered this woman, usually so full of energy and vitality.

But this did not last; soon the reaction set in. How astonished would her urbane guest have been, had he been gifted with second sight, and now beheld the elegant, nonchalant *grande dame* whom he had left lazily lounging in an arm-chair, toying idly with a cigarette.

All eagerness and excitement, she feverishly opened her desk, and ran through the few notes she had taken of Eugen's report as to the Tsarevitch's disappearance, and Count Lavrovski's pusillanimous behaviour. Every now and then short, jerky sentences found their way, half audibly, through her tightly clenched teeth; they were, as it were, the safety-valves of this intense, inward excitement.

For what a chance of complete secrecy had fate thus placed in her way. She shuddered as she recollected that hateful moment on the Austrian frontier, when, through blunder or over-officiousness, alien hands had come across her reports. Oh! the humiliation of it, the mockery of obsequious civility, palpably directed towards a dangerous enemy, a spy of the Russian government. Then, the heavy hush-money, paid with a liberal hand, and yet evidently wholly inadequate to stop chattering tongues from propagating-oh! a mere whisper-the interesting fact, that Madame Demidoff, the *élite* of Viennese society, the friend of princes, kings, and cardinals, derived her great wealth from money paid to her for spying on her countrymen abroad. Some such news did get about, there was no doubt of that; she had felt vaguely conscious of it sometimes, or was it the merest fancy? At any rate there had been no certainty, and certainty there must not be, for Madame Demidoff loved her life, the gay, glittering court life, with the admiration her beauty and wealth aroused, and the friendships her bright wit and fascinating manner attracted around her.

Her profession? Ah! as to that, English readers, try not to be too severe. Russia is a great, but hard mistress, who demands of all her children work according to their means and ability. The word spy has an ugly meaning with us, we loathe it, if applied to a man, and cannot even conceive it as an attribute to a young and gifted woman. But in Russia, where all round an absolute monarchy a web of intrigue and conspiracy is woven, where blows are aimed and dealt at the head of the State from every quarter of the Empire, from every class of society, and always from the dark, these blows must be met with counter-blows of the same nature, secret, swift, and dark. An enemy, hidden behind every pillar of a palace, can but be fought by means as secret as his own. Russia employs them to protect herself and her autocratic ruler: blame the system if you will, and then try to pity its often unwilling servants.

Madame Demidoff never allowed herself to reflect as to whether her calling was worthy of praise or blame, she served her country to the best of her ability, and continued coquetting with the world, whilst daily risking its contempt.

However, on this occasion, fate evidently meant to be kind; the moment she heard his Eminence recount the interesting history of the Emperor's candlesticks, her bright wit had laid itself out for a means to obtain possession of those mysterious receptacles. In a few moments the Cardinal would be back with his precious burden, and surely she had carried through more difficult bits of diplomacy, than that of inducing the Nuncio to entrust her with the mission of conveying the candlesticks across to Petersburg.

This report, merely a matter of a few notes, taken by herself from Eugen's scanty account of the Tsarevitch's disappearance, woud lie easily concealed in the secret receptacle. It was not much, but as, no doubt, it would reach the government sooner than any communication from the conspirators, it might be of some value. Madame Demidoff, well versed as she was in matters of this sort, felt convinced that the Tsarevitch's abduction must have been carried through with a view to making some imperious demands, whilst he was a hostage in the conspirator's hands. She arrived very near the truth, whilst thinking the matter over, and felt at the same time how helpless the Russian police, nay, the Tsar himself, would be, whilst Nicholas was a hidden prisoner.

That Count Lavrovski, who had been-perhaps innocently-very much to blame in allowing his charge to slip through his fingers, would endeavour to recover his traces, by every possible and impossible means, there was certainly no doubt. Viennese detectives were known throughout Europe for their astuteness, and, moreover, a man like this Furet would not arouse the suspicions of the plotters in the way that an agent of the Russian government would. But Madame Demidoff had set her resolute mind the task of being the chief instrument in unmasking the daring conspiracy. She knew what high value her government set on her powers, and this was the greatest opportunity she had ever had of showing how worthy she was of their trust.

She was an absolutely fearless woman. while engaged in the fulfilment of her duties, any danger to her personal safety at the hands of revengeful plotters held no place in her thoughts; but there was the weak point in her armour-was there ever human nature without such a point?– and that weakness lay in her intense dread of being branded before the world, before all the friends she had made, as a spy.

The name gave her a shudder, when, as it were, it stood up and rose before her, as it had done that terrible time on the frontier, when the catastrophe seemed imminent, and the bare thought of hearing it whispered round her, by those who had held it an honour to be counted among her guests, was at times overpoweringly intolerable.

Perhaps in the pride of the woman of society, dreading to be forced to step down from her pedestal, there was much of that deeply hidden sentiment, that changed this worldly politician into a mere woman at times; the sentiment that invariably brought into her eyes that look of wistful tenderness, which she so rarely allowed to dwell therein. Perhaps when she thought of the exalted and high-born friends, who would turn their backs with scorn on the paid spy of the Russian police, did she dwell lingeringly on the one friend, the dreamy, aristocratic young Pole, who thought, alas! so little of her now, but who would scorn her, oh! so completely, then.

But now, if only fate favoured her but a little longer, if she succeeded in inducing the Cardinal to allow her to take the candlesticks over herself to Petersburg, she need not have the slightest fear of discovery. She had looked through the papers, the reports she wished to take; if the secret receptacles were as his Eminence had described them, she could defy the most meddlesome officials on her perilous journey across the frontier.

She heard once more the rumble of wheels; his Eminence's carriage was stopping under the portico. A hasty glance at her mirror reassured her that no trace of either agitation or sentiment was visible on her face. Relighting a cigarette, she once more lounged back in her *causeuse*, and when three minutes later his Eminence entered, carrying his precious burden, he could read naught but ardent curiosity in his fascinating hostess' expressive eyes.

With her dainty fingers she helped him to undo the numerous wrappings which Iván Volenski, so little while ago, had so trustingly wrapped round the valuable *bibelots*.

The enthusiasm of the connoisseur was apparently boundless, and Madame Demidoff was untiring in the praises she bestowed on the charming *bibelots*.

"But, oh dear me!" she sighed, "how brittle!"

"Not so brittle as you may imagine," said his Eminence, "for, after all, these candlesticks are some three hundred years old, and they must have been handled by scores of hands, and are still in perfect condition."

"Not *quite* perfect, I think," she replied, "for see! this one little Cupid has his arm sadly chipped from wrist to elbow."

"Oh, *mon Dieu!*" said his Eminence, "I do hope this has been done before, and not since I have had charge of these inconvenient things. I assure you, *chère madame*, they are a source of constant anxiety to me, ever since his Majesty forced them into my hands. Pray, do allow me to place the damaged candlestick on one side, or perhaps you will extend your kindness by wrapping it up once more in its coverings. I dare not touch it for fear of damaging it further, and can show you the secret spring in the other, for they are both alike."

Tenderly, as if it were a child, his Eminence, with Madame Demidoff's help, had wrapped the damaged candlestick up in its many coverings once more, and had carefully placed it on one side. And now the fair Russian was eagerly watching the Cardinal's fingers as he pressed on the tiny gold leaf, and explained to her the mysteries of the secret spring and the hidden receptacle, so complete, so perfect, so absolutely free from any possibility of detection. Madame Demidoff could ill conceal her excitement, and she nerved herself now to the task, the intricate bit of diplomacy that still lay before her.

"Ah!" she said at last, "no wonder your Eminence feels nervous and ill at ease with such fragile things in your keeping. You have no idea how careless the custom-house officials and railway porters are in Austria, with boxes and valises belonging to men. With ladies' things, I notice, they are much more careful, for they fear the consequences of a crushed gown, or a torn piece of lace."

"You absolutely give me the shudders, *chère madame*," said his Eminence. "I declare my life will be a perfect misery until the happy moment when they are safe in the Princess Marïonoff's hands, let alone the fact of my bitter disappointment in having to forego my long-projected holiday."

Madame Demidoff was still attentively examining the pretty *bibelots* as she said playfully:

"Would your Eminence really care to give up the chance of being Cupid's messenger?"

"If I only knew the way to do that, *chère madame*, how gladly would I do it!"

"Well, then, your eminence shall see what a good friend I am to you. I will take charge of this parcel for you while you are on your holiday, and I promise you it shall be as safe with me as it ever was at the Hofburg."

"You, madame?"

"Yes. I was starting for Petersburg to-night, as you know, and if you like I will take the candlesticks with me, packed up among my best Court gowns and laces; then, if you wish, I will either leave them at the Marionoff palace, with your card, or keep them until your arrival, if you prefer to deliver them actually yourself."

"Madame, you are a thousand times too kind," said his Eminence hesitatingly. "I really hardly like to take you at your word, and yet ——"

"It would relieve you of a great anxiety, is it not so, and, moreover, will leave you free to start on your incognito travel, and not to disappoint those who wished to accompany you," she added archly, noting how ready his Eminence was to yield.

"Ah, madame, do not tempt me, lest I might accept," he said, still resisting for form's sake.

"Say no more about it, then, and accept my friendly offer as it was meant," she said, as, with a charming gesture, she stretched out her hand towards the Cardinal, who gallantly kissed the tips of her dainty fingers.

"How can I thank you, *chère madame?*" he said, with an unmistakable sigh of relief, as he finally gave in to her kind persuasion.

"By telling me all the latest scandals about my best friends," she said laughingly, settling herself once more comfortably in her luxurious armchair.

The victory was gained, and for the next half-hour his Eminence's sprightly conversation helped her to forget the agitations of the evening. He finally took his leave, leaving the *bibelots* that had caused him so much annoyance safely in her charge; and it was agreed that Madame Demidoff would take care of them until his Eminence's return from Carlsbad, when he would hand them over himself to the Princess Marïonoff.

Thus it was that her diplomatic gifts had once more stood her in good stead; and, what she considered the safest possible hiding-place for her reports, was now in her possession to make use of as she wished.

It was getting late, and she was more resolved than ever to leave Vienna this very night, lest his Eminence might change his mind on the morrow and rob her once more of her precious charge. She collected the notes she had recently made, together with a few other papers, containing her various reports to the Third Section; and, unconsciously imitating Volenski's actions, she touched the secret spring and slipped the documents into the velvet-lined receptacle within the shaft of the candlestick. Safe they were, of that there was no doubt.

She carefully packed up the precious *bibelots* in their numerous wrappings, wrote on the outside covering in bold letters: "The property of his Eminence Cardinal d'Orsay-China-Very fragile," then took the parcel up with her, and put it away in her valise.

An hour later, accompanied by her maid who carried the fateful burden, she drove away to the Nordbahn, *en route* for St. Petersburg.

At about the same time Iván Volenski, hearing the Cardinal's footsteps in the rooms below, knocked at his Eminence's door to inquire if he would require his services again that night.

"Come in, Iván," said the Cardinal in highly elated tones; "this time it is good news I have to impart to you. We shall both have our holiday, my son; and I start for Carlsbad to-morrow."

Iván stared at his Eminence in complete astonishment.

"But...what about the candlesticks?" he asked breathlessly.

"Ah! that is the delightful piece of luck that has happened," explained his Eminence. "Madame Demidoff, who is herself going to Petersburg to-morrow, has consented to take the tiresome things over for me, and to keep them in her charge until my return from Carlsbad. I fetched them away myself this evening, and I am thankful to say the responsibility of travelling with those brittle things is safely off my shoulders."

Volenski had become deathly pale.

"Madame Demidoff...the candlesticks...." he gasped. "I do not understand —— "

"Why, my friend, don't look so scared. I was showing the *bibelots* to madame, and quite casually mentioned that I was somewhat disappointed at having, on their account, to give up a long-expected holiday: so she very kindly offered to take the candlesticks over to Petersburg for me, which offer I gladly accepted; and you see me with a burden less on my mind."

Volenski was vainly trying to regain his composure.

"And did your Eminence show Madame Demidoff the secrets of the candlesticks?" he asked breathlessly.

"I really do not remember," said his Eminence. "I dare say I did; but you seem very anxious about the matter. I don't understand the reason."

"My anxiety is entirely in your Eminence's interest; my fear is lest the candlesticks are really safe in a lady's keeping."

"Is that all?" said his Eminence somewhat drily, and darting a quick glance from his penetrating eyes at Volenski, who bore the scrutiny bravely. "You may set your mind at rest, then; *I* consider the candlesticks quite safe, my dear Volenski. So now good-night. I start early to-morrow morning.

"You will, I am afraid, have to stay another day longer, in order to see to the correspondence; but after that your time is your own, till we meet at Petersburg on the 3rd of next month. Good night, my son."

Volenski bowed low before the Cardinal, and, more dead than alive, he reached the quietness of his own room, where he could collect his thoughts and view the immediate future.

That the peril was deadly, that after this at any hour, any moment, the blow might fall, he realised in one moment.

All the papers relating to their plot-so carefully planned, so daringly executed-the draft of their manifesto to be placed by Taranïew in the Tsar's hands, documents which in most cases bore the names of the conspirators, and which would send them, one and all, if discovered, to Siberia or to death, all were contained in the secret receptacle of one of the candlesticks, that even now were in Madame Demidoff's hands. All that required no reflection; they were hard, undeniable facts.

What *did* need serious thinking-as the catastrophe had by some extraordinary stroke of good luck so far been averted-was how to ward it off successfully.

In the first place, it was quite evident that so far the papers were safe.

The Cardinal and Madame Demidoff had seen nothing; either his Eminence forgot or forebore to show the lady the secret spring, or, having done so, he happened to have used the candlestick that did not contain the secret papers. But women are naturally curious, fond of toying with trifles, and any moment —- Volenski's thoughts refused to travel further; the consequences were too appalling. And then again, should he warn his comrades at once of the catastrophe? own to them that the trust they had placed in him he had even the first day betrayed? Would that serve any purpose? What could they do, even if they knew the worst, but calmly await events? For wherever they went, however they hid, it would be impossible to escape the far-reaching arm of the Russian police. No; far better let them remain in blissful ignorance for a time; if the blow was to fall they would know their fate soon enough.

Hour after hour the young Pole sat, his head buried in his hands, trying to think of some plan, some means of intercepting those candlesticks, of robbing Madame Demidoff; but how?–how?

All night he paced up and down his room; it was broad daylight before he fell into a troubled sleep, and in his dream chains were on his wrists, he and most of his comrades were tramping through a dreary desert of snow towards the distant mines of Eastern Siberia, where death awaits the exile-certain, creeping death, a lingering torture that sometimes lasts three entire years.

Chapter VIII

WHOEVER has travelled in a first-class carriage of an Austrian State railway has learnt to know the acme of comfort and luxury that can be conveyed on wheels. True, that whilst the traveller gains in the matter of softly cushioned seats he loses in that of speed; but what would you? This is Eastern Europe, and the Oriental looks upon hurry as one of the seven deadly sins; so the railways he constructs never exceed forty miles an hour, but the springs of the carriages are balanced to a nicety, and everything is done to render the passenger's prolonged stay in the *coupé* a pleasant and luxurious one.

But oh! there is one great, one very great drawback to travelling in those Eastern countries! Who has not known the annoyance, the worry, the bustle attendant on the necessary custom-house examinations at the frontier? Both at Passau, at one end of the Empire, and at Oderberg on the other, the weary traveller is usually landed an hour or so before sunrise. The imperious rules of the Austrian custom-house demand that every article of luggage pass under the inspection of its officials, and that under no circumstances a passenger be allowed to remain in his or her carriage, probably lest he or she may thereby succeed in keeping concealed the very articles of contraband, most strictly taxed by the Austrian government.

"I don't think we need get out, Rôza," said Madame Demidoff in a sleepy voice from the corner of her *coupé*, as the express drew up at Oderberg, the frontier station. "You saw the luggage registered through to Petersburg and loaded, did you not?"

"*Oui, madame!*" replied the maid, looking out of the carriage window; "they are opening all the doors and making everybody get out, but they did tell me in Vienna that, if we have the luggage registered, it can go through without examination."

"Anyway, I shall not get out; put my valise and dressing-bag close to me, and go and order two cups of coffee at the buffet, to be brought here."

"I think madame will not be disturbed," said the maid as she opened the carriage; "everyone has left the platform, and I see no more officials about. I hope madame will be all right whilst I am gone; I will be back directly."

And Rôza prepared to get out of the coupé.

"Excuse me, mademoiselle," said a voice, as she alighted on the platform, "everyone must get out here."

A man, in the uniform of the custom-house officials, stood by the carriage door, respectfully lifting his cap as he peered into the *coupé* and saw Madame Demidoff surrounded by her luggage.

"Surely it is not necessary," said madame in a tone of annoyance; "my luggage is registered through, and they told me distinctly in Vienna that I shall not be troubled with these stupid formalities."

"I am very sorry, madame, but our orders are very strict, and we are not allowed to let anyone remain in the carriages, nor any luggage," he added emphatically, pointing to the valise, dressing-bags, and rugs that lay on the cushioned seats.

Madame Demidoff knew enough about officialdom to be well aware that it was absolutely useless to disobey or even to protest. The man was perfectly civil, nay, respectful, but at any sign of resistance he would call for help, and deposit madame's luggage, without hesitation, on the platform, or carry it away to the customs hall, where she would perforce have to follow it.

Resigning herself with an impatient sigh, she prepared to step out of the carriage, leaving Rôza and the man to follow with her things. She knew she had nothing that she need mind being handled by the most prying Austrian official; her reports and papers this time were safe in the secret receptacles of the Emperor's candlesticks; these she had placed in her valise, labelling them conspicuously: "China-Fragile-the property of his Eminence Cardinal d'Orsay." The parcel might be opened, with a view to verifying the truth of the label, but no one could guess that a Russian agent's reports were hidden inside such brittle works of art.

The whole thing was merely a matter of annoyance and weariness, and Madame Demidoff soon found her way to the customs hall, followed by her maid and the polite but tiresome official, who were carrying her things.

Her large trunks were lying in the hall; these, having been registered, were not opened, but marked with the Austrian custom-house stamp, as allowed to pass the frontier unmolested.

"Have you any bags or small luggage besides, madame?" asked an officer who had been turning over Rôza's bag, and undoing the bundle of rugs and umbrellas she had placed on the counter.

"Yes! I have a valise and a dressing-bag. Rôza," she said, "open them; here are the keys."

"I was not carrying madame's valise or her dressing-bag," said the maid; "the customs offficer was carrying them; I don't see the things just at this moment; he must have put them down somewhere."

"Find them at once. You had no right to let anyone touch them; you know I never allow anyone to carry my bag but yourself."

Madame Demidoff found it difficult to control her agitation, and Rôza peered anxiously round, trying to recognise the official who had charge of the precious bags.

"Did you say a customs official was carrying the things?" asked a porter, seeing the girl's distress; "it is such an unlikely thing for any of them to do, they are all too busy in here."

"He is not here at this moment," said Rôza; "it was a young man with a long brown beard and curly hair; he was in uniform."

"Every one of the officials connected with the custom-house is in the room at this moment, miss; I have known them all for years, not one is missing. I am beginning to be afraid you have been tricked by one of these clever robbers, who have done a deal of mischief before now at these customs stations; you see it is so easy to rob people here, especially ladies, as —- "

"Rôza," gasped Madame Demidoff, who had overheard the man's last words, and now felt sick with terror, "look again! you must have been mistaken.... Where is my valise?... You are responsible for my valise... I shall accuse you of theft, unless you find my valise.... I shall —- "

She checked herself just in time, for an amused and interested crown of spectators began to assemble round her and her maid, eager to watch this elegantly dressed lady so completely losing her self-control over the loss of some small articles of luggage.

The second bell had already sounded; the passengers were preparing to resume their seats in the express. Madame Demidoff, seeing the piercing eyes of one or two officials fixed searchingly at her, felt the necessity of pulling herself together. Her long knowledge of the world-the official world-told her of the danger of betraying too much emotion over apparent trifles, lest those trifles became thereby an object of suspicion. Regaining her *sang-froid*, she turned to the porters, who stood gaping round, and said with calmness:

"My valise and dressing-bag contained some very valuable jewellery. I will give a thousand guldens for their recovery, two thousand if I have them back before dawn. In the meanwhile one of you take my luggage to a cab, and I shall be glad to know the name of the best hotel in this town, where I shall stay until my property is recovered. I must interview the police at once, that is, I suppose, as early in the morning as possible."

"Rôza," she added, turning to her poor discomfited maid, while her orders were being promptly and noiselessly carried out, "here are a month's wages, and the money to pay your fare back to Vienna; do not ever let me set eyes on you again."

After that she walked gracefully and steadily across the room, got into a cab, and was driven to the hotel, while poor Rôza was left to be consoled by the kind porter, until the next train started back for Vienna.

Chapter IX

In the meanwhile Iván Volenski had suffered terribly. His was a peculiar position at that moment. Anxious as he had been to serve the great cause, he had imperilled it-unwittingly-almost beyond recall. His comrades had trustingly placed their lives, their freedom in his hands, lured by his promises of immunity, and twenty-four hours later he had placed them all in the hands of an agent of that very police they so justly dreaded.

And yet the Nuncio, in the morning following that eventful night, had succeeded in somewhat reassuring him. Perhaps his Eminence felt a trifle guilty in the matter of those candlesticks, and thought his secretary was blaming him for allowing them to pass out of his hands. He took great care to explain to Iván the accident to one of the Cupid's arms, which both he and Madame Demidoff had noticed, and which finally decided him to accept her kind offer. Little by little Volenski gleaned from the Cardinal a minute account of all that passed between him and the fair Russian, on the subject of the Emperor's candlesticks.

He heard that Madame had, with her own hands, packed the damaged *bibelot* and placed it on one side, and had herself professed to take the utmost care that not the slightest accident should happen further.

Here was a reason, clearly, for once more thanking Providence that it should have guided his hand towards the damaged candlestick, when secreting the fateful papers.

Madame Demidoff so far knew nothing, that was a reasonable hope, and as soon as his Eminence had left Vienna, which unfortunately would not be till the evening, Iván meant to travel to Petersburg without delay, and on behalf of his absent master ask Madame Demidoff to remit the candlesticks to him, for safe custody within the walls of the Papal Legation.

In the meanwhile not a word to his comrades. He had seen the president the evening before and told him of the alteration in the Cardinal's plan, which would enable him, Volenski, to deliver the papers in Taraniew's hands two days before the anticipated time. To tell them all of the dangers they were in would be unnecessary cruelty.

What could they do but wait for the blow, if it was destined to fall? Mirkovitch would wish to kill the Tsarevitch. It would be revolting to murder a defenceless prisoner.

Now his Eminence had quieted his anxieties. There was no fear, no hurry. After the Cardinal left, Volenski's peace of mind enabled him to sleep quietly, without harassing dreams of prisons and Siberia.

He felt alert and well the next morning, read to take the express through Oderberg to Petersburg, little more than twenty-four hours after Madame Demidoff, following closely on her footsteps.

He breakfasted cheerfully, as one free from care, and with mechanical hands opened the morning paper to glance at the news. And when he read it, there was that in the paper that crushed all his hopes, and for the first time led him to doubt that it was Providence who watched over the Socialist cause.

> "Yesterday, during the examination of passengers' luggage at Oderberg, at six o'clock in the morning, a daring robbery was committed.
>
> "As Madame Demidoff, a lady well known in our aristocratic circles, was alighting from her *coupé*, a man, disguised in the uniform of our customs officials, offered to carry her dressing-bag and valise. He appeared to be following her with her belongings, and it was not till nearly a quarter of an hour later that Madame Demidoff realised that the man and all her belongings had disappeared. It is stated by the lady herself, that the valise contained some valuable articles; her extraordinary agitation on hearing of her loss was much commented upon. The matter is in the hands of the police, who already have an important clue."

What this announcement in the paper meant to Volenski the reader will easily imagine. After the comparative peace and security of the last few hours, the blow seemed to fall on him with almost stunning vigour.

For fully ten minutes he sat there staring into vacancy, unable to think, to plan, his brain almost refusing to take in the fact and all the terrors it conveyed. But a few hours ago those papers, which he had with so light a heart confided to what he felt sure was the safest hiding-place he could devise, had, by some mysterious help of Providence, escaped the eyes of the most astute woman in Russia-unknown to herself she was carrying the secrets of a band of young Nihilists safely across the Russian frontier in the teeth of the police-she, an agent, a spy herself.

The situation was hazardous. Volenski had trembled that some remote chance might at the eleventh hour play him false, but the chance was so slight a one, that he had even the heart to laugh inwardly at the curious coincidence that caused a police agent to be the means of conveying Nihilistic papers across the border. Moreover, in two days at most, he would once more have regained the papers, hand them over to his comrades, and, when all was safe again, laugh at his own terrors. But now how terribly was the situation altered. The fateful papers at this moment were at the mercy of thieves or receivers of stolen goods, who were sure to make the most profitable use of their find; for the secret of the candlesticks could not remain one for long, once they fell into the hand of bric-à-brac dealers, so expert in these matters. And Iván shuddered as he thought how completely in the power of scoundrels he and his comrades would presently be. Would the papers be used for blackmailing, denunciation, or what?

The valet had come in some little while ago, to warn the secretary that it was fully time to start, if he wished to catch the Kassa-Oderberg express, but Iván had impatiently said that his plans were changed; he was not starting that morning.

When the man had left him, and he was once more alone, he again took up the *Fremdenblatt*, and read the fateful article through and through, till his aching temples bbegan to throb and the letters dance before his burning eyes, till he felt dizzy and faint with that most awful terror-the terror of the unknown.

"The police have an important clue," he muttered. "What clue? and what would happen if they did discover the stolen goods?"

The valise, of course, would be opened, and all the articles identified and handed back to Madame Demidoff, who would after that probably only be too glad to give the candlesticks back to Volenski, and shift all further responsibilities from her shoulders; but in the meanwhile they would be handled by dozens of pairs of hands: the thieves first, then the police, then the officials, any one of whom might chance upon the secret spring; and then —- ?

Volenski tried to persuade himself that this chance was very remote, the secret receptacles very ingeniously hidden, the springs very stiff, and only liable to yield after a great deal of pressure; but still a restlessness now seized him, he felt unable to sit still, the crowded streets seemed to lure him, and vaguely he had a hope, that from the groups at the cafés he might hear fresh news new developments of this robbery, that was sure to set all tongues wagging and discussing.

He took his hat and made his way down the Kolowrátring towards the opera house. Instinct-the instinct of self-preservation—whispered to him to control himself, not to let any passing stranger notice his curious agitation, his wild, haggard look. He sauntered into one of the larger cafés, exchanging handshakes and greetings here and there. It seemed strange that not one of those he met referred to the robbery at Oderberg. Volenski could not understand that an event of such immense magnitude to himself should seem one of such utter indifference to others. The new opera, the expected cabinet crisis, Gallmeyer's latest success, were all discussed around and with him, but no one seemed to think the theft of Madame Demidoff's valise of the slightest importance, and Volenski dared not bring the subject up himself; he feared lest his voice would tremble, his anxious eyes betray his agitation.

Hungrily he listened for news, for comments, and went from one café to another, but only once did he hear an illusion made to the robbery; one young fellow said to another that no doubt Madame Demidoff had already succeeded in putting the police on the track of the thieves: she was so expert in police matters herself. The other young man laughed, and the subject was dropped.

The hours passed slowly on; the enforced inactivity weighed heavily on Volenski's mind. The strain of weary waiting for some unknown catastrophe that might be close at hand was beginning to tell on him, and he left the busy streets of the city for some more remote, less frequented spots, where he might allow himself a little more freedom, his agitation a little more scope.

Thus his wanderings had led him towards the publishing offices of the Fremdenblatt, outside which a great amount of bustle and noise proclaimed the sending out of the first afternoon edition. Inwardly thanking the chance that had led his footsteps in this direction. Volenski purchased a copy of the paper and eagerly scanned its contents.

Ah! there it was! some news evidently!

"THE ROBBERY AT ODERBERG

"Our frontier police have once more displayed the wonderful insight and promptness of action for which they are justly noted. The actual thief who stole the dressing-bag and valise of Madame Demidoff at Oderberg yesterday morning was arrested in a private room of the 'Heinrich Marshall' public-house in that same town, where he had taken refuge with his accomplice, in order to divide the booty. As the police forced their way into the room the two thieves were apparently quarrelling loudly over some of the trinkets, which were scattered all over the place. The man, a notorious character, who has long been 'wanted' by the police, seemed in too high a passion, or else too scared, to attempt to flee, but his accomplice, who by the way is a woman, succeeded in gathering a few articles together and effecting an escape through the window. She was, however, recognised by one of the police, and no doubt by now is also under arrest.

"The police were greatly aided in their discovery by two or three of the porters at the station, who, it is said, were stimulated by the large sum of money offered by Madame Demidoff as a reward. Great, therefore, was the dissatisfaction and indignation amongst them when the lady, under the pretence that one or two valuable articles were missing, refused to give any reward till those articles were found. She appeared much agitated on giving her evidence before the magistrate, and explained this agitation on the grounds that one of the missing articles was a pair of very valuable antique gold and china candlesticks, which were not her property, but which were entrusted to her special care by a friend, whose name she refused to disclose. The lady's singular excitement throughout the hearing of the case is causing much comment."

The paper dropped from Volenski's hand, and he stood in the street staring into vacancy, almost staggering, as though he were intoxicated. The terrible thing about this whole drama that was being enacted around him was the fact that, though he was the person most concerned in its developments, it was absolutely futile, nay, dangerous, for him to take the slightest part in it; and not the least of his sufferings was this feeling of utter powerlessness to do aught that could tend to save his comrades and himself from the terrible, crushing blow that might at any moment annihilate them all. But the time for serious deliberation had now arrived; it became absolutely imperative-Iván felt this-that he should trace himself a line of conduct, adopt some plan, decide how far he would warn his comrades, and perhaps seek their help and advice. But for this, quiet was needed, and Volenski now retraced his steps towards his hotel, feeling, moreover, that he had no right to neglect his Eminence's business and correspondence, as, alas! he had but too long done. On his way home many a conflicting thought chased another, many a surmise, a problem, the solution of which might mean life or death to his friends and himself.

Having locked the door of his study, Iván set himself resolutely to the task of chasing away all thoughts of his worries, and devoting himself to his master's work. He wrote what letters were necessary, sorted those that would require to be forwarded to his Eminence, arranged the papers that related to work done, and it was not till late in the afternoon, when the valet brought him a light, that he allowed himself the leisure of once more reverting to the all-engrossing subject of the missing papers, and gave himself the time for thinking over his plans.

The strict adherence to his duties had done him good, both mentally and physically; his brain seemed more clear, his nerves less on the quiver, than during those hours he had spent wandering idly and restlessly in the streets.

Clearly, the situation at this moment was no worse than it had been in the morning, and there was, as yet, no occasion to alarm his fellow-conspirators by telling them the facts of the case, and turning their wrath upon himself, who already had so much to bear.

No, it was better they should remain in ignorance a little longer, for Iván had not abandoned the hope that the papers were still undiscovered, and that he could, after the terrible fright she had had, induce Madame Demidoff to give the candlesticks back to him as soon as she had recovered them from the police. The danger, the sole danger throughout, lay in the fact that papers so terribly compromising should be, if only for a short time, so hopelessly out of his reach, that so deadly a secret should lie at the mercy of so mere a chance.

As for his Eminence, Volenski well knew that, as soon as he was free from diplomatic duties, he never even glanced at a newspaper; his name, so far, had not been mentioned, and —- But here a fresh, a curious train of thought arose in Iván's mind, and the darker side of the picture-he had vainly tried to look upon as bright-presented itself before his mind. Why had the Cardinal's name been so studiously kept back by Madame Demidoff? Was it merely that, very naturally, she did not wish him to know how badly she had failed in her trust, or was there-and Iván paled at the thought-some reason for her wishing that his Eminence should not hear of her loss, some reason for the curious excitement into which, woman of the world as she was, she had betrayed herself, to the extent of arousing the comments of the magistrate and the reporters?

Had she, perchance, already discovered the dreaded secret, and, wishing to claim the honour and glory of her find, was she anxious to recover the papers, and, with them in her hands, denounce the conspirators and claim her reward? Was her agitation the outcome of her terror lest she should lose the precious proofs, without which, perhaps, her memory might be at fault in naming the perpetrators of the daring plot? Ay, all that was possible. Iván knew it all the time, strive though he might to lure himself into the false belief that all was sure to be quite safe so far. Madame Demidoff was evidently staying at Oderberg, ready to claim her property at once. Iván pondered if he should communicate with her; a sensible proceeding enough, if she had not discovered the papers, but worse than useless if she already had done so. One more chance now lay open to Iván, and that was to approach the police himself-now that the candlesticks had actually been mentioned as part of the missing property-and find out if they would allow him to claim them, on behalf of his Eminence the Papal Nuncio.

With that object in view, late as it was, he ordered a *fiaker*, and drove off to the headquarters of the Detective Department. The chief of the police, Baron de Hermansthal, he knew well, having frequently met him in society, while in attendance on Cardinal d'Orsay. The baron was a busy man, very busy, and he kept Volenski waiting three-quarters of an hour in his ante-room; Iván had plenty of leisure, therefore, to decide what line of diplomacy it were best to adopt.

He would tell Baron de Hermansthal, under an official seal of secrecy, that the candlesticks alluded to by Madame Demidoff, in her account of her missing property, were none other than those entrusted to her by his master, Cardinal d'Orsay; that these antique candlesticks were to be unofficially presented to a lady resident in Petersburg, by the Papal Nuncio, on behalf of an exalted personage whom Volenski would not name, but would leave Baron de Hermansthal to guess. Finally, he would add that his Eminence completely relied on Baron de Hermansthal's well-known tact and discretion, and that both the Cardinal and the exalted personage would desire that the matter be kept as far as possible from further publicity, the candlesticks not pass through any hands that were not absolutely necessary, and that it was to further this object that Volenski, on behalf of his Eminence, now claimed Baron de Hermansthal's powerful assistance.

This plan and speech well formed in his head, Iván, feeling more calm, was able to enter the private room of the chief of the Austrian police, even without a tremor.

Baron de Hermansthal, a quiet, aristocratic-looking old man, with a charming eighteenth-century manner, listened attentively to all Volenski had to say, asked him to take a seat, while he would look over his notes relating to the case, and after a few moments:

"My dear Volenski," he said, "I should be very happy under the circumstances to help his Eminence in any way that is within my power. If you will tell me what you would wish me to do, I might see in what way I can be of most assistance to you."

"I merely want your permission to claim the candlesticks on behalf of his Eminence, without their passing through any hands, save yours and mine, and without all the formalities that usually attend the claiming of property found by the police."

"But Madame Demidoff is for the time being the person from whom these candlesticks have been robbed; she might object to their being handed over to anyone save herself."

"Madame Demidoff has declared before the magistrate that they are not her property," replied Volenski. "I will communicate with her as soon as I have your authorisation to do so, and you will find that she will be only too glad to hand over to me all responsibility in the matter."

"That will be for her to decide," rejoined the chief of the police drily; "we can discuss the matter later on; anyhow, I can promise you that I will communicate with you the moment the police have seized the missing articles."

"They have not yet been found, then?" asked Iván breathlessly.

"They are not actually in our possession," corrected the chief of the police.

"May I ask what that implies?" asked Volenski, whose parched lips and quivering nerves hardly enabled him to frame an intelligible query.

"It implies that we know where they are, and that we can lay our hands on them at any moment."

"And —- "

"Stay! let me explain," added the polite baron kindly, as he noted Volenski's eagerness. "The police are, as you know, well acquainted with the woman who was in the room with the thief at the time of the arrest, and who ran away through the window with a part of the booty. She is one of that class whom it is *bon ton* to designate as the 'unfortunate.'"

"Yes! I knew that the female thief had escaped, but I should have thought —- "

"That our police, usually so active, when there is a little rough-and-tumble work to do, would not fail in overtaking and capturing her. That would have been done, no doubt, but for a very important reason, which is this: the officer in command, once having recognised the woman, knew that he could lay hands on her at any moment. She lives in Vienna, and haunts every *cabaret* and third-rate hotel, her favourite resort being the 'Kaiser Franz.' He therefore intends to lull her into false security, with a view-by keeping a constant watch on her movements-of discovering and bringing to justice a gang of receivers of stolen goods, who, so far, have completely baffled our vigilance, and whose tool we believe her to be."

"You think, then, that the woman brought those candlesticks to Vienna with her?"

"We know she did, for she was seen in Vienna this very morning, and is being closely watched."

"Surely your Excellency will give immediate orders to have her rooms searched this very evening?" said Iván imploringly.

"I have no objection to doing that," said Baron de Hermansthal urbanely, "as I am anxious to prove to his Eminence how willing I am to serve him."

"Your Excellency will allow me to accompany the police?" asked Volenski eagerly.

"To identify the candlesticks," he added, seeing that Baron de Hermansthal shook his head in emphatic refusal; "there may be others there."

"On one condition, then, that you do not interfere with our men in the discharge of their duty, merely pointing out the articles you claim as your property, and that you allow the officer on duty to bring them here, to my office, without opposition.

"To your office?" said Iván.

"Yes! I shall have to insist that the candlesticks remain in my charge until I hear definitely from you or Madame Demidoff herself that she wishes them handed over to you."

"And in the meanwhile?"

"I promise you faithfully that no one shall even touch them; you shall yourself see the parcel locked in my desk, and I shall be delighted to give them up to you, as soon as I am satisfied that Madame Demidoff has no objection to my doing so."

Iván reflected a moment. In his mind there at once arose the idea that chance would certainly favour him, once he actually had the candlesticks in his hands; he had but to press the spring while the police were searching another part of the room, and he could, he felt sure, extract the papers unperceived. There were so many eventualities that might happen, between the time when the candlesticks were found and the moment when Baron de Hermansthal would finally turn the key of his desk on them; so many opportunities, any one of which would find him on the alert. His hesitation, therefore, lasted but a moment; the next, he had assured the amiable baron that he would strictly adhere to his instructions, and was quite willing to wait for Madame Demidoff's decision, once his fears that the candlesticks might be too much tampered with had been allayed.

"In the name of his Eminence," he added diplomatically, "I thank your Excellency for your courtesy in the matter."

"Pray say no more," replied Baron de Hermansthal, as he touched the bell in order to give the necessary instructions.

"Tell Serjeant Meyer I wish to speak to him," he said to his valet.

"It is very late," he added, looking at his watch; "nearly eight o'clock, but that is no matter, as no doubt you will find the woman has gone out on her nightly errands and left you the coast clear."

A discreet rap at the door and the serjeant appeared, saluting his chief.

"Meyer," said His Excellency, "do I understand that the woman Grete Ottlinger has, so far, not been caught trying to sell the stolen property?"

"No, your Excellency; she has not left her rooms since this morning, when she arrived from Oderberg. Two of my men have been stationed outside her doors all day, and she has not gone out. Her *concierge* thinks she has been in bed all day. She drove this morning direct from the station to her room, and had then a large-sized box with her."

"Very good! I wish you now to take one other man with you and go to the woman's room, with this warrant to search all her premises. You will seize all the suspicious property you can find. If the woman is there you may arrest her, if not, your men will be having an eye on her, and she can be arrested when she comes home. Monsieur here has my permission to accompany you and to identify certain articles that belong to him, and which you must then bring back here to my office. Do you understand?"

"Yes, your Excellency!"

"*Au revoir*, then, my dear Volenski," said Baron de Hermansthal, turning to Iván; "I shall expect you here with the candlesticks according to your promise, on which I rely."

And His Excellency, rising from his seat and dismissing the serjeant with a nod, thereby intimated to Volenski that he had done all his duty allowed him to do, and that the audience was at an end.

Iván once more was profuse in his thanks. Fate indeed favoured him; it was now for him to seize the splendid opportunity with skill and promptitude. He felt in his pocket-book that he was well provided with money; a *douceur* to the serjeant, should he chance to see what Volenski did not intend, might be necessary.

Five minutes afterwards he was in a *fiaker* with Serjeant Meyer and another member of the corps, and in his heart of hearts he hoped that the next half-hour would see his precious papers transferred once more to the inner pocket of his coat.

Chapter X

It was in a narrow street, in one of the most squalid quarters of Vienna, that the *fiaker* stopped, after some ten minutes' rattle over the cobbled streets of the city.

Serjeant Meyer jumped out, followed by Iván and the other police officer, and casting a quick, searching glance along the apparently deserted street, he walked unhesitatingly under one of the wide porticoes in front of him. The house was one of a row of tall buildings, ugly, square, and straight, with a balcony running along outside the first-floor fronts the whole length of the street, and a wide, open *porte cochère*, leading, through a square courtyard, to the lodgings at the back of the buildings. There was a lodge for the *concierge* on the right, at the foot of the wide stone staircase that leads up to the front of the house, but no one guarded the apartments that overlooked the courtyard; there was nothing there worth guarding, the inhabitants belonging mostly to the very poorest classes of Vienna, who had nothing worth stealing.

A group of women, with untidy hair and dirty aprons, stopped their chatter and nudged each other significantly with great, coarse, bare elbows, as they caught sight of the police uniform; and one or two heads appeared at some of the windows, as the heavy steps of Serjeant Meyer and his followers echoed on the stone pavement of the courtyard.

Having reached the dark and narrow staircase leading to the floors above, Serjeant Meyer turned to Iván.

"I do not see either of our fellows anywhere about, so I conclude the woman has gone out."

"So much the better," said Volenski; "we need have no disturbance, then; I suppose the people of the house are used to this sort of thing, for they took very little heed of your uniform or our presence."

The serjeant shrugged his shoulders, intimating that he cared little for any disturbance that might arise, and he added:

"This house is one of the worst famed in this part of Vienna; it is almost entirely tenanted by women of Grete Ottlinger's class. A police inspection of their premises is a very frequent occurence, and the inhabitants have, I think, one and all, spent some time in prison or hospital."

The three men now began cautiously ascending the dark stone stairs, guiding themselves by the narrow, iron hand-rail, and feeling their way with utmost care. Serjeant Meyer, who was in front, seemed to be very sure of where he was going, for it was without any hesitation that he stopped somewhere about the fifth floor, and, crossing a dark passage, tried the handle of one of the doors that opened thereon.

The door, however, seemed to be locked, and after one or two repeated loud knocks, the serjeant applied his broad shoulders to the feebly resisting timber, and broke it open without any difficulty.

The room, in which the three men now found themselves, was but dimly illumined by a glimmer of light that came in through the window from the courtyard below. The serjeant struck a match and lighted his lantern; the aspect of that room then presented itself in all its squalor and hideousness: an iron bedstead, covered with a ragged, coloured counterpane, stood out from the centre of the wall opposite; to the right as they entered, an earthenware stove with the tiles mostly cracked and loose; then a coarsely painted chest, the drawers of which were mostly open, displaying a medley of dirty laces and faded ribbons; two or three chairs in a rickety condition propped against the walls, and a table with a broken ewer and cracked basin, completed the furniture of this abode of misery and degradation; the floor was bare, the boards unwashed and rough; on the window-sill stood a mirror and two or three pots of powder and cosmetics, while on the chest of drawers lay a litter of papers and two or three faded photographs.

Iván stood gazing round in horror. It had never been his misfortune to witness the type of misery, sordid and abject, that was depicted by this bare room, by the tawdry scraps of ribbon, the half-empty, evil-smelling pots of cosmetics, and his mind reverted to the exalted notion he and his comrades had of the "people," of the poor, who were in the future to frame laws and rule empires, the "people" about whom they talked so much, and knew so little, the "people" whose men and women lived like *this*.

Then, pulling himself together, he gazed blankly round him. Save for that chest of drawers, which appeared half empty, he could see nothing wherein the Emperor's candlesticks could have been hidden, and a cold perspiration stood on his forehead as he turned to Meyer and asked him what course he intended to pursue.

The serjeant once more shrugged his shoulders; then, pointing to the bed, he ordered his man to turn the *paillasse* over.

"Would you like to search that chest of drawers?" he smiled, sarcastically addressing Volenski. "My impression is that the bird has flown and taken her treasures with her."

Iván waited not for a second offer; he was already emptying the drawers, throwing ribbons and rags in a confused heap on the floor. Hope was fast dwindling away; this golden opportunity, from which he had expected so much, was proving futile. The splendid chance he would have had in this dark room, if only the candlesticks were to fall in his hands, was not to be his after all. Half fainting with the closeness of the atmosphere, and the nerve-strain consequent on the bitter disappointment he was experiencing, Iván dared not let the serjeant see his face, frightened lest the astute detective should notice his strange agitation, and jump at conclusions, which he might afterwards communicate to his chief.

"It seems to me," said Meyer at last, "that we are wasting our time here; the woman has evidently taken with her what valuables she had stolen, either because she is always prepared for a police raid during her absence, or she may actually have gone to dispose of them. Anyhow, monsieur," he added, "with your permission, we will leave the matter for the present, and report proceedings to the chief."

Iván had completely emptied the drawers, and was now impatiently turning over the letters and papers that were lying in a confused heap on the top of the chest. A half-torn, almost wholly faded photograph had riveted his attention. A somewhat coarse, large featured woman's face, with dark, provoking eyes, and a wide, laughing mouth. He wondered, as he looked at it, whether this was the woman who held his fate and that of his comrades in one of those clumsy, low-bred hands, and whether he would ask Serjeant Meyer if this was Grete Ottlinger.

"Is this the woman?" he asked at last, with sudden determination, turning towards the police officer and holding out the photograph.

"Yes! it is," replied Meyer, after a hasty glance. "No beauty, is she?" he added, with a laugh.

Then the other man having opened the door, the serjeant stood, evidently impatient to be gone, his lantern in his hand dimly lighting the dark passage beyond. Volenski with a sudden impulse slipped the photograph into his pocket, and throwing a last hopeless look at the squalid abode he had entered so full of hope, followed Meyer down the narrow stairs.

He was loth to give up all hope; his was a sanguine and buoyant disposition, that refused to give way to despair. A plan had already formed in his brain, a confused idea that would require the quietness of the deserted streets to order and to organise.

"As we have not found anything belonging to me up there," he said to Serjeant Meyer, as the latter prepared to step into the cab that was waiting for them outside, "I don't think there is any necessity for me to follow you to His Excellency's office. What do you think?"

"You know best, monsieur, of course," replied Meyer. "I have a very short report to make about the woman's absence, together with every article of stolen property; also the fact that our two fellows are no doubt on her track, as I do not see them anywhere about. His Excellency must then decide, if it is worth while going to the 'Kaiser Franz' to-night on the chance of finding her there, or leave the matter alone till her return."

"I should think the latter is by far the wisest course," said Iván hastily; "however, that is none of my business. Will you tell his Excellency that, as my property has not been found, I will call on him again to-morrow morning, and in the meanwhile will communicate with Madame Demidoff?"

Serjeant Meyer and his assistant bowed to Iván as they stepped into the *fiaker*. Volenski waited a few moments till the sound of the wheels died out in the distance, then, taking a cigarette from his case, he lighted it with great deliberation and sauntered off towards the Ringstrasse with an anxious but determined look on his young face.

Chapter XI

Poor Volenski had begun to look very haggard and careworn; the mental strain of the past few days was beginning to tell upon him. He was paying less attention to his dress, there was an absence of elasticity in his step, and an almost furtive look in his usually so frank, if dreamy, eyes. He realised this, as, having reached the brilliantly lighted cafés that enliven both sides of the Opern and Kolowrátring, he caught sight of his own figure in one of the tall pier-glasses beyond the windows of the shops, and noticed the untidy look of his cravat, the dusty appearance of his clothes. He looked at his watch; it was barely nine o'clock-time enough to pay a flying visit to his hotel and remedy the obvious defects of his toilet, before he sallied forth to accomplish the task he had in a moment's resolution set himself to do.

It was with the greatest care that he proceeded to change his clothes for the conventional black and white of evening attire, not forgetting the bouquet in his buttonhole, nor the fine handkerchief peepinig from the pocket of the coat. He wished to look the perfect type of the young man about town, idle, elegant, and gay–a rôle he had played so much during the greater part of his life that it had become second nature; and especially he wished to leave absolutely behind him all traces of the harassed conspirator, who feels himself tracked, and dreads at every turn to meet his doom.

There was no doubt that since the fatal moment when the candlesticks were stolen on the Austrian frontier, fate loomed dark against him and his friends, and he had been alone to face the dangers and difficulties, to battle against relentless chance. The most adverse coincidences had surrounded him from the first, and when luck appeared to be on the turn, some untoward, wholly unforeseen event occurred, to dash any hope he may have had to the ground. First the Cardinal's unfortunate idea of entrusting Madame Demidoff with the candlesticks, then the robbery at Oderberg, next the escape of one of the thieves wiith the very articles that were of such paramount importance; finally the one grand opportunity he would have had to-night, but for Grete Ottlinger's wonderful luck, or foresight, in taking the booty along with her.

But from all this chaos of mischance the unfortunate young man had gleaned one fresh ray of hope. He hardly dared to trust to it, but it gave him the inestimable boon of being able to act for himself, to be actually employed in trying to rescue himself and his friends from the terrible position into which his well-meant blunder had led them. It meant that with tact and diplomacy all was not lost yet, and that in the meanwhile he would at least be free from the intolerable torture of inactivity, waiting, wearily waiting, for that crushing blow that might descend at any moment.

As it was getting late, and Vienna was in the full swing of its usual evening entertainments, Volenski found his way to the "Kaiser Franz," a brilliantly lighted but tumbledown-looking hotel in the Muzeumgasse, which had been named to him by the police as the usual nightly haunt of Grete Ottlinger. Everyone who has been to Vienna, probably, has noticed this hotel, with its flashy front, decorated with masses of gilded plaster, broken and tarnished, and its showy-looking porters in threadbare knee-breeches that show signs of once having been of crimson plush, and gold-laced coats that but too plainly proclaim the second-hand wardrobe dealer's shop. It is mostly very noisy from within, especially in the small hours of the morning.

Under the portico, which is always very brilliantly lighted, usually stand half a dozen of so very young dandies about town, with their opera hats, worn at the backs of their heads, and a full-flavoured cigar between their teeth, more with a view to giving them an air of maturity than for actual enjoyment. They scan the over-dressed, over-painted, mostly somewhat faded beauties that pass up and down the street in front of them, waiting for an invitation for supper and champagne, and do so with an air of nonchalance that would fain betray the habits of a *roué*.

It was with this crowd of young men that Volenski mixed, though he had the greatest horror, usually, both for the scanners and the scanned; but to-night he stood under the gaudy portico, watching the very unattractive bevy of yellow-haired beauties that passed in front of him, as if he expected to find the idol of his heart among that crew.

He had taken the precaution to inquire of one of the porters if Grete Ottlinger had gone within, and being answered in the negative, he also cocked his hat at the back of his head and proceeded to light a cigar, trying to look as unconcerned as he could, while he waited for *her*, the original of the photograph he had so providentially found in that uninviting garret-her, whose confidence at that moment he would have purchased with her weight in gold. Would champagne, or unlimited cognac loosen her tongue, he wondered.

Still they passed; some of them were accosted and taken in to supper, others tried by a smile to encourage the diffident. They all looked very much alike, Volenski thought; they might all be sisters, in fact, as they were sisters in shame and misery.

But *her* he would recognise. He knew it, he would know her among a thousand. He had only looked at her photograph one minute, but her face danced before his eyes; ugly, commonplace as it was, was it not the face of his destiny?

Ah! there she comes at last. Iván seemed to feel her presence even before he actually heard her harsh, ill-bred voice, and recognised her coarse, low-cast features under the shadow of a cheap, gaudy hat.

Even before he had time to speak to her she was close up to him; no doubt she had noticed how intently he had been watching her. He threw away his cigar, and trying to look amiably at the poor wretch, he beckoned to her to follow him.

She surveyed him up and down, took in at a glance that the cloth of his coat was of the finest, his linen irreproachable, and his cigar fragrant; this evidently leading her to the conclusion that there would be plenty of money spent on the supper, she nodded a careless *adieu* at her less fortunate companions and followed Volenski into the hall.

Iván was at the bureau ordering a private room, and the most *recherché* supper, and choicest champagne the "Kaiser Franz" could boast of. The waiters, obsequious and attentive, were addressing congratulatory nods to Grete at the gold-mine she had evidently come across, and very soon Volenski and his companion were ushered into a gaudy, showy apartment on the first floor.

The windows opened on to the Muzeumgasse, and Volenski leaned out into the cold night air, trying to cool his throbbing temples and calm his quivering nerves.

The presence of that common, showily-dressed woman made him feel uncomfortable. He could not chase from his mind the vision of that garret, up a squalid stair, with its bare floor, rickety bed, and drawers full of dirty, tawdry knick-knacks. He tried to think of her only as the one being who could, if she would, if he set the right way to work, save him from his perilous position.

She had evidently hidden the candlesticks in some secure spot, away from the eyes of the police, or, maybe, had already sold them to an accomplice. To find this out was his self-imposed task, and the few moments that elapsed before the waiter returned with the supper, Iván spent in steeling himself to the ordeal.

For a trying ordeal it would surlely be to a young and refined man, unaccustomed to the coarser pleasures of the gay city. Iván in turning round caught the woman's eyes fixed with an amused, half-pitying expresesion upon him. Clearly she thought him a young, shy fool, anxious to taste the cup of dissipation, but with a lingering awkwardness when brought face to face with it. The part suited Iván; he determined to play it, and hide his nervous irritability under the cloak of intense shyness. He did not even know what type of conversation was expected of him, but he trusted that the champagne, which he had ordered dry and plentiful, would loosen his own tongue as well as hers.

Grete had employed the last few moments in divesting herself of her cloak and hat, and she now appeared in a gaudy evening dress, displaying charms that, like the Emperor's candlesticks, had the value of antiquity.

"Leave everything on the sideboard," she said to the waiter; "we will wait on ourselves, and you need not come till we ring for you."

The waiter, well trained, arranged the supper-table as directed; then, taking a last look round to see that everything was in order, he discreetly withdrew.

"I hope you will like what I have ordered," said Iván awkwardly; "if not, please ask for anything you want, anything that will make you lively, you know," he added, with a forced laugh; "we must enjoy ourselves, Grete, mustn't we?"

The ice was broken. Grete burst into a merry peal of laughter.

"Well, you are the funniest creature I have ever come across," she said, shaking with merriment. "Are you afraid of me? You have not opened your mouth since you brought me here. No, not there," she said, as Iván solemnly sat down opposite her at the table; "I call that most unsociable, and I give you my word I won't eat you up. *Ach! Herr Je!*" she added, with a sigh, "the things on the table are much more appetising than you, and you are not the first young gentleman I have supped with. Come and sit here, little booby," and she placed a chair close to her own.

Iván, glad that she started a conversation-which she was evidently well able to conduct by herself-changed his seat as she wished, and poured himself and her a full glass of champagne.

Poor soul! she was enjoying the *recherché* supper thoroughly, and, after the first glass of Perrier Jouët, began telling him anecdotes of her chequered career; a quarter of an hour later she sidled up to him, looking somewhat amused the while.

"You funny booby," she laughed, "you may, you know," and she stretched out a very red cheek towards him.

"Look out! the waiter is coming," said Iván pushing back his chair and hastily jumping up from the table.

The bare idea of having to kiss that ugly, elderly woman sent a cold shiver down his spine.

"What if he is, booby mine?" she replied, giving way to an uncontrollable fit of laughter-the idea seemed so amusing. "Do you think he has never seen me kissed before? Come, cheer up, sit down again; your mammy shan't know. There now, this is much more comfortable," she added, for Volenski, on whom the importance of the present situation flashed again in an instant, had offered his feelings as holocaust on the altar of the great cause, and resumed his seat beside the donna-with an arm round her antiquated waist. She placed her yellow head languishingly on his shoulder.

"Do you know, little booby, that, as a rule, I don't much care for young gentlemen like yourself?"

"No?" he asked indifferently.

"Well, you see," she said, with a pout, "it is difficult to get any fun out of them; they are so mortally afraid of being seen in our company that they won't take us anywhere."

Iván could not help smiling to himself at the idea of taking this beauty-say, to the opera-and meeting his Eminence on the way, and did not wonder that Grete was not very often taken to the theatre by "young gentlemen" like himself.

"Who are the people you like best then, Grete?" he asked, in order to keep up the conversation.

"Oh! I have many friends-real friends," she said. "But that's a fine ring you are wearing, booby!"

Volenski felt at this moment that it was of the most vital importance that he should hear something of Grete's real friends; he must get her to tell him about them; surely the accomplice, the one who was arrested at Oderberg, was one, and, who knows, another might at this moment be actually in possession of the fateful candlesticks!

Taking the ring off his finger, he slipped it into Grete's hand, and said with an effort at cordiality:

"Pray accept it; it will adorn your pretty hand. But do tell me some more about your friends-the real friends that were not young gentlemen?"

"One of them was an actor, and earned quite a lot of money-he used to play all kinds of parts-and, Lord! sometimes now, he makes me laugh with the clever way in which he can disguise his handsome features. Never mind, my pretty one," she added coaxingly, "you have got a nice little face of your own too, and —- "

"Never mind about my face; tell me about his."

"Now you are angry," she said, with a pout. "I shan't talk any more about him, though he *is* a clever chap! I could tell you one or two of his tricks. But there, that's nothing to do with you."

Volenski felt the conversation was becoming interesting. He swallowed the last vestige of repulsion he felt for this coarse, now decidedly intoxicated, woman, and pouring her out a large tumblerful of champagne, "Drink this, my girl," he said, "and tell me some of your friend's tricks. I should like to hear something that will make me laugh."

She drank the champagne and said nothing for a few moments, then burst into a loud laugh.

"Ah! but I did the best trick of all to-day; I tricked them all, every one of them; they thought themselves mighty clever, they did, but Grete Ottlinger was one too many for them. Booby, don't look so scared; give me another glass of champagne, and I'll tell you all about it. Another glass, booby; fill it to the top. I don't often get champagne; men mostly only give me beer or spirits. You see, I am not so young as I was. But champagne—I love champagne —- "

She was getting very tipsy and very noisy. Volenski, no less excited than herself, tossed down a couple of glasses. He felt nothing, he was conscious of nothing, except that in five minutes he would know his fate, and that this woman held it in her hands.

"Oh! it was funny," she laughed again; "I knew they were after me. I am no fool. They let me come back to Vienna; they meant to search my rooms while I was out; they thought I wouldn't know.

"Booby," she whispered, "old Moses Grünebaum was waiting at the station for me. He had the things already in his shop, while the crew were following me round the town and turning out my rooms; and they will find nothing. Ha! ha! ha! what a lark, booby! Eh, booby? What's the matter with you? Here! I say, booby, what on earth are you after?"

For Volenski was fumbling for his hat, his gloves, his coat, and, tossing a hundred guldens to the woman, he had fled from the hotel, past the astonished waiters into the streets, leaving Grete to pay for the supper, and still muttering to herself: "Booby-well I never! *Gott in Himmel! Ach, Herr Je!*"

Chapter XII

How Iván ever reached home that night, without being arrested by the police on suspicion of being drunk, he never afterwards could say. He remembered nothing after the time when, out of Grete Ottlinger's confused babble, he had gleaned the name of Grünebaum-the name that to him at last meant absolute salvation. He knew the shop well on the Opernring, kept by old Moses Grünebaum, and containing a wonderful collection of antique jewellery, furniture, and curios of all kinds-a shop much frequented by connoisseurs, the most thought of in Vienna, in fact, for that class of things, certainly not one that would ever fall under suspicion of harbouring stolen goods.

It was obviously too late to interview old Moses at that hour of the night. Iván, though hardly alive to any outward facts, save the all-absorbing one, was nevertheless conscious of that, and instinct guided his reeling footsteps to the hotel on the Kolowrátring.

A mass of letters awaited him; correspondence he was sadly neglecting in these days of anxiety. One of them was from his Eminence. Iván tore it open in eager excitement. It ran as follows:

KLINGER'S HOTEL, MARIENBAD,

28th *February*.

"MY DEAR SON,–You will see by the above address that I have altered my plans and am staying here for the present. The fresh mountain air is having a most beneficial effect upon my health, and I shall probably stay (D.V.) the full length of my intended holiday. I hope you are getting on satisfactorily with the work fast enough to enable you to take some days' rest before we once more meet at St. Petersburg for diplomatic business. By the way, if you should happen to get there before I do, I think it would be as well if you would call on Madame Demidoff, and ask her to hand you over the Emperor's candlesticks, which then could remain in your charge. I hope she accomplished her journey in safety, and that not the slightest harm has come to those tiresome things, which very nearly succeeded in depriving me of my holiday. I assure you, my dear son, when I think of all the enjoyment I should have missed on their account, I am doubly grateful to madame for the kind favour she has done me.

"My apostolic blessing on you, my son, and sincere respect to Madame Demidoff when you see her.

"ANTONIUS D'ORSAY,

Cardinal-Archbishop."

Volenski put down the letter; a sigh of complete relief came from his heart. Thank Heaven! his Eminence knew nothing. It was not to be wondered at; the robbery at Oderberg had not created much comment in the press owing to the speedy capture of the thief, and it would have been nothing but the most adverse coincidence if his Eminence, who, to Iván's knowledge, never glanced at a newspaper, should that one day of all days have seen the two numbers that contained an account of the theft.

He knew from his own experience that the facts were not sufficiently mysterious to excite public interest, and as his Eminence's name had not once been mentioned by Madame Demidoff, it was not very likely that the Cardinal would hear of the matter from any outside source. Madame evidently did not mean that his Eminence should hear about her loss-that was only natural; no one likes to own to gross carelessness, least of all a lady. Oh! that he might only get rid of the fear that already she knew all, and was on the same quest as himself, backed by Russian money and Russian influence! But even then, at present, he was ahead of her. She had not interviewed Grete Ottlinger, she could not know where the candlesticks were, and before

Grünebaum's shop was open the following morning he meant to be on the spot, ready to pay away all he possessed for the priceless receptacles of the secret papers.

That night, as he well knew that sleep would never come to him, he spent in getting through all arrears of work for his Eminence. He meant, as soon as he had seen Grünebaum and purchased the candlesticks, to start at once for Petersburg, and deliver the papers to Taranïew. Three days had now elapsed since the abduction of Nicholas Alexandrovitch; three days, during which Iván, absorbed in the harrowing search for the missing messages, had not seen his comrades. Every day added one to the many dangers of discovery, and Dunajewski and his comrades were still pining in the Moscow prisons.

Oh! this burden of responsibility seemed too hard to bear; the terrors of carrying the secret papers seemed as nothing compared with what he had to undergo. But, thank God! all these anxieties would be over by to-morrow at the latest, and then in his heart of hearts there first occurred to Iván the wild longing to give up all these intrigues and plots; be content to live the life of a quiet citizen, and leave Russian politics steadily alone.

The busy night he spent acted soothingly on Iván's nerves. He worked until the tardy winter's dawn peeped in through the curtains, then, having refreshed himself with a bath and a good breakfast, he once more sallied forth on his quest, and nine o'clock found him on the Opernring, outside Grünebaum's shop, waiting to see the shutters taken down.

The moment that was done he stepped in and asked to see the proprietor.

A snuffy old Jew, with flat nose and broad lips, with eyes like a toad's—so nearly dropping out of his head, that he appeared to be wearing spectacles for the sole purpose of keeping them in their sockets-came forward, rubbing his hands benignly one against the other, evidently wondering who his very early customer could be. He was accustomed to mistrust everybody.

"A very good morning, sir; and what may I have the pleasure to show your Excellency to-day?–jewellery?–antiques? —- "

"I have come on a matter of private business," said Volenski briefly. "You had better show me into your office, for your own sake."

The Jew looked at him keenly for a moment from behind his spectacles, then said suavely:

"I have no business that I should wish to conceal; but if your Excellency will take the trouble to walk this way —- " And he led the way to a well-lighted, luxurious little office at the back of the shop, where a quantity of voluminous ledgers and cash books testified to the extent and prosperity of his business.

"Will your Excellency be pleased to be seated?" he said.

"No, I prefer to stand; what I have to say won't take long. You received yesterday, at the station of the Nordbahn, a parcel of goods from a woman named Grete Ottlinger. These goods were stolen. You knew it. What have you to say?"

"That I am as innocent of this as a newborn babe, your Excellency; that I was never out of my shop all day yesterday, it being, as your Excellency no doubt will deign to remember, a very rainy day; that I never even heard of any woman named Grete Ottlinger; that I never set eyes on stolen goods-this I swear by our fathers Abraham, Isaac, Jacob, and by the grave of my forefathers."

"Enough of this drivel," said Volenski impatiently; "you lie, and you know it. Now I will be brief with you. Among that stolen property —- Don't interrupt me," he said sternly, as the Jew made another attempt at protest, and raised his hands upwards as if calling Abraham to witness of his innocence; "I said that, among that stolen property there was a pair of antique china and chased gold candlesticks. I wish to know where those candlesticks are. I will pay you the full amount you will have to give to Grete Ottlinger, and two thousand guldens besides, if you will hand them over to me at this moment. If you refuse, I will lodge information against you at the police, and within half an hour you will be arrested, your house, books, and belongings searched, and even if nothing definite can be proved against you-you might be a cunning rascal-your business will practically be at an end. You will be marked as a suspicious person, and none of your customers will dare return to you for fear of buying stolen property."

The Jew, who at the beginning of the interview had turned pale to the lips, had now regained some composure. Rubbing his two hands together again:

"Now I see that your Excellency is a generous gentleman," he said benignly, "with no desire to harm a poor old man, who has wife and family to support-but with a wish to deal fairly with him. I swear to your Excellency that my greatest desire is to serve you in every way I can, and I will tell your Excellency the whole truth. I have never done such a thing before, but the woman tempted me, and the things were very beautiful. I did not like to keep them in my shop-it wasn't safe-and as soon as I received them from Grete Ottlinger I packed them off, and sent them through a trustworthy messenger to my partner in London. I received a telegram from him this morning to say he had crossed the frontier quite safely last night, and is now out of reach of the police, who are still busy hunting for the things in this city. And if your Excellency will keep to your word, and give me ten thousand guldens, which will only be one thousand over and above what the candlesticks have cost me, I will tell you where my partner is to be found, and then it will be your Excellency's own fault if you cannot succeed in inducing him to part with the articles in question."

"I will pay you nothing till I have the candlesticks in my possession, then I pledge you my word that you shall be paid in full. Now choose quickly, you have no time to lose; the express starts from Vienna at one o'clock; if you give me your accomplice's address, together with a few lines on a card, telling him that I am a friend, I will leave for London at that hour; if you refuse, I go this instant to the police and lay information against you."

"How do I know that you will not lay information against me when once you have secured the goods?" the Jew muttered suspiciously.

"Look at me," said Volenski; "do I look like a vile traitor who would use a man first, and betray him after?"

The Jew shot a piercing glance from his bleary eyes at the young Pole, whose manly face looked fierce, agitated, passionate, but certainly not false; and, without another word, he took from his pocket-book a business-card, bearing the words-"Moses Grünebaum, Dealer in Antiquities," wrote on the back-"Isaac Davies, 14, Great Portland Street, London," and below, "To introduce a friend," and handed it to Volenski.

"I shall be back in Vienna on Saturday," said the latter, "and if I bring the candlesticks with me, I will bring you the money I promised on that very day."

And, pulling his hat over his eyes, Volenski walked out of the shop, taking no further notice of the Jew, who followed him to the door, bowing obsequiously, and still irrelevantly calling to Abraham, Isaac, and Jacob to witness to his complete innocence.

Chapter XIII

ON arriving at this hotel Volenski found a telegram from Baron de Hermansthal, asking for his immediate presence at the detective office. Wishing to avoid anything that might in any way seem suspicious, he went at once, although he had ceased to care now what the police were doing in the matter; whatever they did, could not affect the candlesticks, as he would be in London long before the promptest investigations could possibly lead to the discovery of Grünebaum's agent abroad. Baron de Hermansthal had, however, quite a great deal of news for him; the night before, the woman Grete Ottlinger had been arrested outside the "Kaiser Franz" for being drunk and disorderly, and had been induced this morning, by the examining magistrate, to reveal the name of Moses Grünebaum, a well-known dealer on the Kolowrátring, as the receiver of all the stolen property she and her accomplices brought into the city. The man would probably be arrested that afternoon.

"I thought you would be relieved to hear this," the amiable baron added; "if you like to call at my office later in the day, I might give you a special permission to view the suspected articles in Grünebaum's shop, and if his Eminence's candlesticks are among them, and the police satisfied as to your claim to them, they might be handed over to you in the course of a few days."

Oh! all this bureaucracy and red-tapism, how thankful Volenski was that he was independent of it! A few days indeed! time to allow Madame Demidoff, who naturally would be communicated with at the same time as himself, to claim the candlesticks as part of *her* stolen property. In a few days Volenski hoped to be in Petersburg, back from London, the fatal papers handed over to Taraniew, and then his own connection severed from the brotherhood. To that he was fully resolved. The last few days had taught him a lesson that would take a lifetime to forget.

"I am exceedingly obliged to your Excellency," he remarked somewhat drily, "for the trouble you have taken in this business; as I am obliged to quit town for a few days, I will leave the matter now entirely in your hands."

"I don't think you can do better," said Baron de Hermansthal. "It is now merely a question of time, for the property is in the charge of the police, no doubt, along with the other goods in Grünebaum's shop, and I will give strict orders that no candlestick is to be tampered with, till you or Madame Demidoff have identified those belonging to his Eminence."

"I suppose," said Iván tentatively, "that Madame Demidoff has been communicated with?"

He was anxious to hear what her movements had been so far, how near she had been on his track.

"I am expecting Madame Demidoff this morning, as I sent her an official communication, asking her to favour me with a call. She came back to Vienna yesterday, having exhausted all inquiries round about Oderberg, and resolved to let us do what we could on her behalf."

"No doubt, then, she will identify his Eminence's candlesticks," said Iván, much relieved to find that Madame Demidoff could not possibly have seen Grünebaum privately in the short interval that elapsed between his own interview with the Jew and the subsequent police raid.

He took his hat and bowed politely to the amiable baron, as he once more thanked him for his kindness, then took a hasty leave, eager as he was to get away.

The quest after the fateful papers had become an all-absorbing one. Iván Volenski seemed unable to think of anything while he was on this mad chase after the compromising documents. He seemed almost to have forgotten the very existence of the prisoner in the Heumarkt, the comrades at Petersburg, who had not yet heard the news, and those at home, who would be wondering when and how he had started on his important mission, and how soon their manifesto would be placed in the Tsar's hands, and Dunajewski and the other brethren safely across the frontier; little knowing that the entire fabric, on which the Socialist brotherhood rested, was in danger of crumbling at any moment.

And delay...delay was so dangerous! What had Count Lavrovski done? Were the Russian detectives on the track of the conspiracy? Would they succeed in discovering the captive before any important good had resulted from the daring abduction? In any case nothing but disaster to the cause and its followers could ensue while the papers that held all their secrets were in strange hands. To get those back was life and death to one and all, and with that all-absorbing, fixed idea in his mind Volenski, having packed up a few necessaries, was ready to start for London by the afternoon express.

He had plenty of time during the forty hours' journey to England to meditate on the folly of all this plotting and planning, that inevitably led all those who indulged in it into perils of their lives and liberty. He himself, with ample means and a brilliant career before him-what a fool he had been to risk all his prospects for the sake of Utopian ideas, that would take perhaps centuries to develop, but surely could not be advanced by hot-headed *coups* such as Dunajewski, Taraniew, and he himself planned. Would a handful of young enthusiasts revolutionise Russia, when the *moujiks*, for whose benefit they were supposed to plot and plan, were the very last to lend them a helping hand?

Ay! the reform of that great country would come some day; soon, perhaps, as it came in France, violently-sweeping like a tornado a throne, a dynasty before it-but that would be when the people's hour had come, when the nation themselves knew what they were craving for, when liberty had ceased to be a word in the mouth of a few, and had become a desire in the hearts of all. Time, then, for all Russians that had pride in manhood to join in the cause of freedom and attack the throne if it stood in the way, sweep away the powers that be, if they do not tend to the desire of the people. But let it be the people that have that desire; let it be a spark in their heart, placed there by a divine hand, and not kindled slowly and forcibly by the breath of a few fanatics.

Amidst these conflicting thoughts Volenski had reached the English capital. He left his bag at Charing Cross Terminus Hotel, meaning to start back for Vienna that same evening, and, as soon as he had swallowed a light breakfast, he took a hansom and drove to No. 14, Great Portland Street.

This time he was sure of his ground; there was no occasion to exercise any diplomatic skill. He walked straight into the shop, asked to see Mr. Davies, and said in quiet, business-like tones, in fairly good English:

"I noticed in your shop, a day or two ago, a pair of antique china and gold candlesticks that took my fancy at the moment. I hadn't the time to look at them then, but would be very glad if you will show them to me. They were of gold, with very pretty *vieux Vienne* Cupids with bows and arrows. Do you recollect the ones I mean?"

"Perfectly, sir, perfectly. I regret, however, that I cannot oblige you, as I sold those same candlesticks to one of my customers late yesterday afternoon. He is a great collector of curios of all kinds, and, like yourself, sir, was greatly taken with the beauty of the *vieux Vienne* Cupids. But I have some very beautiful candlesticks, both antique and modern, that you might care to look at —- "

"No," said Volenski, whose excited brain refused to take in the Jew's assertion, "I want those particular ones-I must have them-no matter what I pay for them. Here," he added, as he noticed that Davies was beginning to eye him suspiciously, "is my introduction from your Viennese partner," and he handed him Grünebaum's card; "you will see by that, that I am a friend, and if you will deal fairly with me, no harm shall come to you, but if you refuse to help me to regain my property--for those candlesticks are mine-I will find means of setting the police on your track as a receiver of stolen goods. Now bring me those candlesticks at once, and name your price for them. I am in a hurry, as I want to catch a train."

Isaac Davies took his accomplice's card, and turning it about between his fingers, still eyed Volenski with a remnant of suspicion.

"I tell you no harm shall come to you," said Iván impatiently. "I am even willing to pay you a very handsome price for those candlesticks; you see, therefore, that you can but gain by being frank with me. Grünebaum gave me this card, that you should have no fear."

"Sir, I have told you the truth," said Isaac Davies at last drily, adding with an indifferent shrug, "as for your threats, they have no weight with me; I am free from blame. Grünebaum's is a good and well-known firm in Vienna. I have a perfect right to buy goods from him without falling under suspicion of receiving stolen property; I deny that the articles Grünebaum sends me *are* stolen, and I defy you to prove it. Whatever information, therefore, I choose to give you, I do so because my Viennese correspondent has recommended you to me, and not from any fear of your threats or the police."

"Then," gasped Iván, who was beginning to realise that the Jew was telling the truth, and the candlesticks were really out of his reach once more, "those candlesticks are sold?"

"To a Mr. James Hudson, of 108, Curzon Street, Mayfair, a great collector of antiquities and great connoisseur. You may probably have heard of him. No? Well, I sent him those candlesticks to look at yesterday, knowing well that if he saw them, he would take a fancy to them. They were very beautiful things, sir, and if you happen to have anything more of the same class of goods I shall be very happy —- "

"To the point, man. For God's sake, tell me, did he buy them?"

"He did, sir," said Isaac Davies, nettled at this curious customer's impatience. "I knew he would. What is the next thing I can do for you, sir? Nothing? Good morning, sir."

And seeing another client entering his shop, Isaac Davies turned on his heel and took no further notice of poor Volenski, annihilated by this last most cruel blow of all. Ill-luck was, indeed, pursuing him. Every now and then a ray of hope would pierce the darkness of his misery, only to be again dimmed by some terrible difficulty, each of which seemed more insurmountable than the last.

The unfortunate young man was coming to the end of his endurance, and for one brief moment, as he reeled out of Davies' shop, the idea crossed his mind of ending all this misery, once for all, by throwing himself underneath the first omnibus that passed; but it was only for a brief moment, the next he had realised that his death now, at this point, would mean hopeless, irretrievable ruin to his friends and comrades-all the more so as they would be unaware of their danger, completely ignorant, as they were, of the loss of the compromising papers. It was still on his coolness, his pluck, and perseverance that hung the lives of his comrades, and he determined to make one more effort to save them. "The last," he thought hopefully.

His plans now would have to be more complicated, and Volenski gathered all his faculties together for the laying of these plans. He had almost mechanically walked out of the Jew's shop, and, still unconsciously, was turning his footsteps towards Curzon Street. One thing was certain, he must see Mr. James Hudson-any pretext would serve for that-he would think of one later on. What he must think out at once was, what he should say to Mr. James Hudson when he did see him. He knew him well by reputation. He was a man of boundless wealth and boundless eccentricities, generous to a fault, and had been a great favourite with the ladies in Prince Albert's days. No doubt he was a gentleman, and if—- Yes, that was it. The whole interview flashed before his fevered brain as if he saw it on a stage.

Characters: The courteous, benevolent old gentleman, a sort of modern Bayard-Mr. James Hudson. The young man with a past that involved a lady's honour-himself. Scene: A drawing-room in Curzon Street, Mayfair.

The young man with a past: "Sir, you hold in your hands the honour of a lady. Will you give me back the letter?"

Courteous old gentleman: "The letter, sir-what letter?"

The Y.M.W.P.: "It lies concealed in yon candlestick that adorns your mantlepiece. Sir, years ago we were foolish; we sinned, she and I. Having no means of approaching each other, we used the graceful toys as love's letter-box. One of those letters-hers-was forgotten, there-she is now married–I am married-we are all married, but you, sir, hold the candlesticks-you hold her fate! Will you give me back the letter?'

Courteous old gentleman: "Sir, pray take it-it is yours!" Tableau.

There is no doubt that, at this stage, poor Volenski's dreams had become the wanderings almost of a lunatic; his agitated manner, his wild, excited gestures attracted the attention of the passers-by.

He made a violent effort at self-control, and having arrived at No. 108, Curzon Street, rang the bell, and asked for the footman who opened the door whether Mr. James Hudson was at home.

The elegant specimen in knee-breeches, silk stockings, and powdered hair looked down at him from the majestic height of his six feet odd inches, and asked, in what seemed to Volenski very astonished tones:

"Mr. Hudson, sir?"

"Yes; will you please give him my card, and tell him I desire to speak with him at once?"

"Sorry I can't take the card, sir," said the footman gravely, and he added in solemn tones, "Mr. James 'Udson died, sir, this morning, suddenly, at 'alf-past two; death bein' due to hapoplexy, sir. 'E will be buried hat 'Ighgate cemetary on Thursday, sir, at eleven o'clock: no flowers, by request. The 'ousekeeper will see you, sir, if it is himportant."

The voice sounded to Volenski as if it came from very far away-so far, in fact, that it had ceased to have an earthly sound. The man's face began to dance before his eyes, then to whirl past him at terrific velocity, as did the house, the furniture, the windows. He had only just sufficient strength to tell the man to call him a cab, to get into it, shouting to the driver to take him to Charing Cross Terminus Hotel. After that his senses mercifully left him for a time; the poor, tired brain refused to grasp this last calamity, the failure of this last hope. Volenski never remembers how he got to his room at the hotel, or what happened for the next few days, as complete nervous prostration followed the intense mental and physical tension.

The people of the hotel sent for a doctor, who, under the circumstances, felt justified in opening Volenski's pocket-book, and, seeing it well filled with bank-notes and drafts, ordered a couple of hospital nurses and everything else that was needful, which was chiefly absolute quiet and rest.

Chapter XIV

WHILE their comrade was undergoing the various vicissitudes into which his over-anxious zeal had led him, the members of the Socialist brotherhood in Vienna had been going through a very bitter time of anxiety and dread for the future.

A week had now elapsed since Iván Volenski should have, according to his own statement, left Vienna for Petersburg with the papers entrusted to him, and up to this day no message had come from him.

He had promised to give them some definite news of himself as soon as he had reached Petersburg. If all had been well he should have been there three days ago, and must by now have given the papers over to Taraniew. Why, then, did he not wire, or give some account of himself, to reassure them at least that he and the fateful papers were safe?

The night before they had met in their committee-room in the Franzgasse, and it had been a gloomy and agitated meeting. The conviction had first begun to take root in their minds that the usual fate had overtaken their daring messenger, and that after this any day, at any hour, the crushing blow might fall upon them all.

Once their papers were in the hands of the Third Section, probably not one of them could hope to escape. And what was more galling, more bitter even than the fear of death, was the fact that their plot, so magnificently planned, so daringly carried out, would end but in their own perdition, with nothing gained save a gang of convicts tramping to Siberia.

Unless —-

Yes! there was an "unless," a grim and great alternative that, in spite of the president's almost entreating speeches, in spite of the better, more fined nature in most of them, had gradually but surely forced itself upon their minds. Mirkovitch had put it to them five days ago, when flushed with their triumphs they thought of nothing but the great ends they could gain by their success. Now that this success seemed like bubbles, to be bursting before their eyes, they thought once more of their old comrade's grim words, and began longing for revenge.

The president had asked them to meet again to-night, and towards ten o'clock they dropped in, one by one, anxious for news, full of eagerness.

"Has anything been heard?" were the first words uttered by each as they entered, and, on hearing the gloomy negative, pipes were brought out and smoked in sullen silence.

The president had arrived, urbane, temperate, as usual, but even on his face there sat a look of deep apprehension, which he evidently strove to hide from his younger comrades. Every now and then he glanced anxiously towards the door, where Mirkovitch's footsteps would probably soon be heard.

The latter had not yet arrived; yesterday he had seemed more grim, more sullen than ever. Unlike the other members of the brotherhood, his thoughts seemed in no way to dwell very anxiously on Iván and his probable fate; they seemed to tend with ever-growing satisfaction towards the terrible goal, the attainment of which he hoped to reach shortly. He had not yet put into words those thoughts that he knew already loomed darkly in the minds of all, and which completely overmastered him; but he meant to obtain their consent to-night, and felt, as he entered the room and noted the attitudes of them all, that his would be an easy victory. He had taken good care to sow his seeds in good time; to-night he meant to reap the harvest.

Maria Stefanowna was with him. They all trusted her with the secrets of the fraternity now. The part she had so successfully, so discreetly played at the opera ball had shown them that a woman such as she was is often a valuable adjunct in the affairs of men.

The girl came in with her father, and having greeted those she knew best among the committee, she also lighted a short cigarette and waited to hear what they all had to say.

"Mirkovitch, have you heard from Volenski?" asked a dozen eager voices.

"No," he replied; "I thought the president or some of the committee would have had some message from him by now."

There was a silence; then a sullen voice said:

"Swietlitzki declares that the Papal Nuncio did not go to Petersburg at all, but that he has been staying in the Tyrol for the last week."

"But Iván said that he was starting with him on the following day, Ash-Wednesday."

"Surely ——- "

"No!" interrupted the president, "no fear of that."

"Do you mean that he may have fallen into the clutches of the police?"

"That is impossible," said the president reassuringly, "for we should not all be sitting here peaceably. By now every one of us incriminated in those fateful papers-and most of us are so, I imagine-would have been arrested. The very fact that we are still, all of us, free men proves that our papers are safe."

"Our papers might be," rejoined one of the brethren, "but what about our messenger?"

"He might, before being arrested, have succeeded in destroying the papers, you mean," said another.

"I feel sure," asserted one of the older men, "that Iván would sooner part with his life than with our secret."

There was once more silence in the room. Mirkovitch's grim eyes travelled mockingly, perhaps even contemptuously, on those assembled round him. Maria Stefanowna took no part at all in the expression of these various surmises and conjectures. She sat listening attentively to all that was said around her, but her eyes, ever and anon, were attached with a curiously anxious and restless look on her father, who sat opposite to her.

"Does it not strike you, my friends," said Mirkovitch at last, sarcastically, "that it is impossible for us, some eight hundred leagues away, to arrive at any definite conclusion as to what has or has not happened to Volenski?"

That was so, it seemed such a hard and dry fact, and yet there was some slight satisfaction, even in these vague conjectures, shared with one's neighbour, in hearing what the other comrades' thoughts and fears were, and every now and then in provoking a reassuring remark from their calm president.

"For my part," added Mirkovitch, "I think Volenski's silence is exceedingly ominous. There could have been no possible danger in his sending a wire to the president-who is known to be a great friend of his-apprising him of his arrival in Petersburg. If he had accomplished the journey safely you may be quite sure your chairman would have received such a message."

The president looked up anxiously at his comrade and stretched out his hand towards him, as if he would check him from proceeding with what he was going to say.

"Speak, Mirkovitch; you have something on your mind," said one of the committee, and "Let us hear!" came from all corners of the room.

Maria Stefanowna, like the president, made a movement as if she would have wished to stop her father, but, perhaps realising the futility of such an attempt, she resumed her cigarette and her anxious, expectant attitude.

"What I have to say will, I know, not seem pleasant to some of you," said Mirkovitch, who had now risen and looked down on his assembled brethren from his towering height with that contemptuous smile peculiar to himself. "You see, most of you have had the misfortune of having been born gentlemen. I have not, and, therefore, none of those feelings you call refined have place in my burly, low-born mind. My friends, though you may be gentlemen, you must not be weak and effete like those of your class. For God's sake, look the facts straight in the face, and try to forget yourselves and your own petty feelings for the good of our country and our people which we serve. You would not listen to me before, against my counsel you used our mighty, our successful plan for the paltry purpose of getting our comrades out of prison. I tell you," he asserted, bringing his powerful fist down on the table, "that they are all willing over there to die for the good cause. They are not, as we are, fond of life and liberty; they love the cause first, themselves not at all. Why should we care what has happened to Volenski? What is one man against the weal of millions?"

He looked inspired now, a prophet of the Utopia that dwelt in all their hearts, the Utopia at which some of them would have arrived by the most gentle of means, but which this man would conquer by fire and sword.

They all knew what htey would hear next; they knew what Mirkovitch had all through wished them to do. Most of them would willingly have stopped their ears not to hear the dreaded utlimatum that this powerful man would in the next moment hurl at them.

"We have often had speeches here," resumed Mirkovitch once more, "to inflame our enthusiasm against the tyrants that hold our destinies and those of our fellow-men in the palm of their hands. I am no orator; the speeches did not come from me. Some of you, who to-night seem weakest, spoke the loudest then. But I tell you, we have a great weapon in our hands against them, the one weapon that must, sooner or later, lay them prostrate at our feet, asking for the mercy they have never granted us.

"That weapon is *fear*. Let us strike terror in their hearts, my friends; they have no other vulnerable points. When we can, let us strike in the dark, at all times swiftly and surely, so that in days to come, very soon, they will look at each other with blanched faces and trembling lips, and murmur what they dare not say out loud, 'My turn next, perhaps.' It is then, and then only, that we shall be the masters, when cowardly fear will place them grovelling at our feet. Then we can dictate, then we can negotiate, and before then what matter Dunajewski or Volenski, or a hundred such? What are their lives that we should hesitate for a moment to wield the weapon our own efforts have placed in our hands?"

He sat down once more, and a dead silence followed this speech. Enthusiasm was once more kindling in the gloomy faces around, once more the man with the iron will had imposed it on his weaker comrades, and when his mocking eyes again travelled round the room he could read on the faces before him the result of his powerful words; he could read it in the gradual disappearance of the anxious looks, the unspoken terrors; could read it in the young, dreamy eyes, now once more burning with the glow of enthusiasm, the thirst for valiant deeds, at peril of life and freedom.

"Mirkovitch is right," was heard on all sides.

Perhaps some of them still shuddered when they realised what his being right meant to the helpless prisoner in the Heumarkt, but they were very few now, and when the president's anxious eyes and Mirkovitch's triumphant ones scanned all the faces there, they knew that if the grim Socialists's wish was put to the vote there would be many "ayes" and very few "noes."

"After all, my friends," resumed the stalwart Russian, now laying his trump card on the table, "I am sure, if you were asked, you, none of you, would wish to see our great plot come ignominiously to grief through the liberation of our prisoner by the Russian police, and all of us convicted without having attained anything, after having dared so much. Any hour, any minute now, may see us all in the clutches of the Third Section, while Nicholas Alexandrovitch leaves my house free and unscathed. Every second heightens our peril and diminishes the chances of our triumph. At least if we fall, for there seems no likelihood of our being able to escape undetected, let us have accomplished something that will leave our names for ever glorified in the eyes of every patriot in Russia."

Thus was the doom of the prisoner sealed; very little discussion followed. Unwillingly, but still unanimously, they had given their consent to the dastardly deed which Mirkovitch but too willingly offered to do for them. One or two of them asked for a respite-twenty-four hours-during which, after all, some news of Volenski might yet arrive. The old Socialist, satisfied at having carried his point, willingly agreed to wait till the morrow, and a final meeting therefore was convened for the next day, at the same hour. The president had said nothing. What was his influence against that of his grim comrade? The tide of feeling, a mixture of mistaken duty and misguided enthusiasm, had sealed the fate of the young Tsarevitch.

The weight of indecision seemed to have been lifted from the minds of them all. Althought they neither smoked nor chatted, according to their wont, the gloom had quite given place to irrevocable determination. No more questions or surmises were put forward as to Volenski's probable fate or their own certain doom. the word "assassination" had sounded once, pronounced by many lips with a shudder. It was now called "execution"; Mirkovitch, the willing executioner; they, the judges who had arrested and condemned a prisoner just as their tyrants did with the millions over which they held sway.

Half an hour later they were all preparing to depart, sober and silent, with thoughts of the great morrow. No one had taken much notice of Maria Stefanowna, whose large dark eyes had been fixed on her father, as if he held her in a trance. When most of them had gone she also slipped out of the room, not waiting to see if Mirkovitch was accompanying her, as she brushed past him. Out in the street she hailed a *fiaker*, jumped in alone, and was driven rapidly in the direction of the Heumarkt.

Chapter XV

Maria Stefanowna's position in the great Socialist brotherhood was a curious one. The only woman among so many men, she yet knew all their secrets and plans, and, though young, had often been of good counsel to them.

Mirkovitch, her father, had early in life accustomed his motherless daughter to his mysterious ways and curious, weird speeches. Maria had been born and bred in the hatred of the rulers who sat upon the Russian throne, and listened to all her father's sometimes bloodthirsty schemes, not often sharing in them, but always with silent approval.

When the brotherhood, after full deliberation, decided to entrust her with the most important rôle in the abduction of the Tsarevitch, she felt proud and happy at the thought of being for the first time of use to the great cause, which she had just as much at heart as the most enthusiastic among them. When Dunajewski and his comrades had been arrested the girl's ears were filled with horrible tales of the tortures they would undergo, both whilst in prison at Moscow and afterwards during that weary tramp across the snowy desert, with horrible intervals of so-called rest in overcrowded, evil-smelling halting places; then the mercury mines, that in three years change the hale and hearty youth into an old man, palsied and imbecile.

And the cruel fate could be spared them if she, Maria, was clever enough to play the part that had been assigned to her, could lure the Tsarevitch into a prison, not only comfortable, but luxurious, where he would only be kept until those poor martyrs at Moscow were once more restored to liberty and happiness.

She threw herself into the part of the enterprising odalisque, with the finesse and coquetry peculiar to all the daughters of the East, and the next day was able to receive with pride and delight the congratulations and thanks of the brotherhood, assembled to do her honour.

She guessed her father's dark thoughts with regard to the helpless prisoner under his charge, but so far had had no occasion to tremble for his safety. She knew most of her comrades as being of refined and temperate nature, knew the high-minded, aristocratic president, the gentle and dreamy Poles, who were in strong majority, and felt that her father's evil designs would be held well in check.

But when Volenski, the trusted messenger, gave no sign of the success of his mission, when all spirits waxed gloomy and lips began to murmur, Maria's heart began to beat anxiously, both for the safety of the young captive and for the honour of the cause.

The great cause that she revered and worshipped, to which she meant to dedicate her life, was about to be polluted by a crime so foul, so cowardly, that Maria Stefanowna's whole soul rose in rebellion, and imperiously demanded of her woman's wit to find a means of averting so terrible a catastrophe; and it had been she who had led Nicholas Alexandrovitch to what threatened to become an unknown grave. She looked shudderingly at her hands, and wondered if some of the young blood would not leave on them a lifelong stain.

All night she paced up and down her room in restlessness and terror. At times she thought she could hear her father's footsteps creeping stealthily towards the prisoner's room, and then she had to stop her ears not to hear the last agonised cry of the young man, surprised and helpless in the hands of his assassin.

It was broad daylight before her nerves and brain found a short respite from the terrible anxiety that had tortured her, since that last decisive speech of her father's at the meeting last night. Womanlike, she had obstinately pondered till she thought she saw a way out of the difficulty. Being a Russian she was very devout. She prayed long and earnestly for the success of her scheme, which was to save the prisoner from murder, and her comrades, her father, the great cause itself, from eternal shame.

Chapter XVI

IT had been a weary, an anxious time of waiting for Count Lavrovski, while forced to sit patiently at the hotel, watching for news of the truant, and sending reports of the Tsarevitch's imaginary attack of measles to the authorities at home.

But obviously the deception could not be carried on much longer. Already the Tsaritsa had spoken of coming herself to Vienna and nursing her son, and one or two imperious demands had been made through the ambassadors for bulletins, signed by the great physicians, who no doubt had been called in to attend upon the illustrious patient. A day or two more would see the catastrophe, all the more terrible as Lavrovski's deceit would be taken as a sure sign of complicity; and the old Russian now cursed his own weakness in not having immediately shifted the responsibility of this fearful calamity from his own shoulders, which would have been, as events proved, by far the wisest course to pursue. Disgrace would have been the result then-perhaps an order to spend a couple of years abroad; but now he saw no hope before him, only a vision of Siberia, there to end the last years of his life.

He had looked, half shudderingly, half resolutely, at the tiny revolver that would be his supreme and forlorn hope. No doubt, in consideration of his long years of faithful service to the family, his Imperial master would grant him the inestimable boon of death, instead of the slow tortures of a Siberian prison.

Oh! how Count Lavrovski wished he had never consulted that French detective, or having done so, had confided the whole truth to him, for had he not led him into these additional days of deception, which he felt would prove his ruin?

While Volenski, stricken down by his persistent ill-luck, had at last found in physical prostration merciful oblivion from the harrowing anxieties of the past few days, Count Lavrovski, in no less pitiable a plight than the young Pole himself, sat meditating as to whether he would once more seek out the old detective, this time armed with the determination to tell him all, or whether he would send a wire at once to Petersburg asking for immediate help. The latter was undoubtedly the wiser course. Prudence and duty both dictated it, but human nature, ever prone to put off an evil moment to some more distant time, begged inwardly for more delay.

It was, therefore, with a mixture of buoyant hope and surprise that Count Lavrovski heard that a lady desired to speak with him on a matter of urgent business. She had refused to give her name, the waiter said, but had asked him to tell the Count that she was the bearer of a message from M. Furet.

"Show her up at once," said Lavrovski eagerly.

What could it be but good news? Something of importance the detective had heard and wished to communicate with him at once. Count Lavrovski rose as M. Furet's purported messenger entered the room, and bowed instinctively as he beheld a lady of refined bearing-so different from the usual female detective's aid he had expected to see. Her face was closely veiled, but her figure and general appearance bespoke youth as well as refinement.

She took the chair which the old Count was offering her, and dexterously placed it so that her back was against the window, while Lavrovski's face remained in full light.

"Monsieur le Comte," she began courteously, "I must first tender you my humble apologies for the slight deception I have been forced to practise upon you. I wished to make sure of being allowed to see you without delay, and used M. Furet's name as an introduction to your presence. I am not his messenger."

"But, madame-mademoiselle —- " stammered Lavrovski, bewildered at this strange preamble, "I —- "

"You are at a loss to understand," rejoined the stranger, "how I knew that M. Furet's name would be a passport to you. I will tell you that presently, when I have delivered you the message with which I am entrusted, and for which I will venture to ask your kind attention."

Count Lavrovski was too bewildered to reply. There was a slight pause whilst the mysterious stranger was evidently collecting her thoughts, and Lavrovski instinctively felt some dread he could not account for, some undefinable fear that he would hear a message of life and death.

"I think I am right in stating, monsieur," she resumed, "that you are at this moment in grave anxiety concerning the disappearance of an august personage whom I need not name. That is so, is it not?"

Lavrovski had half expected this, and yet he turned pale with emotion when he heard this stranger so calmly talking of this dreaded subject. He did not reply; the lady seemed not to expect it, for she proceeded at once.

"Let me assure you first of all, monsieur, that that august personage is well in health, and for the present in no personal danger."

She emphasised the words "for the present," watching the effect on Lavrovski's face.

"True," she continued, "he is a prisoner at this moment, in a prison at once luxurious and comfortable. But he is in the power of persons-those whose emissary you see before you-who will be only too glad to give him back his freedom."

A look of relief crossed the old Russian's face. He thought he understood it all now. In spite of her sex, her well-cut clothes, and refined appearance this woman was one of a gang of desperadoes, who lived by abducting persons, instead of stealing goods, demanding high ransoms, like wayside brigands. Well! thank God! there was no great harm done, and money in Russia is always plentiful when needed. Count Lavrovski without another word took out his pocket-book, and, laying it down on the table, said simply:

"Name the price."

"It is my object, in coming here to-day, to do so," said the stranger imperturbably; "but I will ask you, Count Lavrovski, to put back that pocket-book—the price of the Tsarevitch's liberty is not contained therein."

Lavrovski stared in mute surprise; every minute of this strange interview plunged him into ever-growing mazes of astonishment.

Then, rapidly and to the point, Maria Stefanowna plunged into her subject. She hardly paused to take breath, she had arranged the whole interview so thoroughly in her mind during those long, harrowing hours she had spent pacing up and down her room last night. She explained to the now almost bewildered old courtier the daring plot that had placed the heir to the Russian throne a helpless prisoner in the hands of a few young enthusiasts. She explained to him her own share in the matter, recalled to his mind the mysterious odalisque, and assured him that the august prisoner's comforts were attended to by herself with the utmost care.

She spoke in clear, well-defined tones, with a briskness that fairly took Count Lavrovski's breath away. The old Russian listened, horror-struck, to the open allusions or covert threats of his Imperial Highness' dangerous position. He heard with amazement how so monstrous a thing had been planned and executed on so sacred and august a personage by a gang of young men whose very existence he had been ignorant of, and he realised at once how futile would have been any effort on his part, or M. Furet's, to fight so many enemies in the dark.

"I think, monsieur, I have now made it clear to you that the Tsarevitch's life is entirely in the hands of those who hold him prisoner, and my purpose in coming here to-day is to tell you on what conditions Nicholas Alexandrovitch shall be restored to life and liberty."

"Conditions, madame? I will hear no conditions," exclaimed Count Lavrovski, who at last recovered his speech at this outrageous audacity. "Death, swift and sudden, shall overtake you, one and all, and those who have sent you. Thank God, the Russian police are far-seeing, far-reaching enough to reach the son of its beloved Emperor, without having to listen to conditions dictated by such as you."

He had jumped up full of wrath, and his hand was already on the bell-pull, in order to summon Stepán to guard this villainous emissary of evil tidings, while he himself sent forthwith to Petersburg for the wherewithal to punish this daring crew.

Maria Stefanowna had sat there unmoved; her foot tapping rapidly on the ground was the only sign of impatience she gave.

"Monsieur, remember," she said quietly, "that if you pull that bell your young master will be dead before another night has passed over his head."

The old Russian understood. What a fool he was! The woman spoke truly. What could he do but wait patiently, meekly, to hear the manifesto of these wretches who held the dagger against a Tsarevitch's heart?

Later, perhaps, revenge might come, but now they must negotiate, treat with them, however galling it might be.

"You are right, madame! No doubt you and your companions know how completely we are in your power, or they would never have dared to send you to me."

Then with a violent effort at self-control he added:

"I will listen to what you have to say."

Maria Stefanowna gave a sigh of satisfaction. She had gained his undivided attention, as well as his confession of the power she held in her hand. The plan she had formed in her mind needed now but propounding; she was sure at least of undivided hearing.

"Monsieur," she said, "although I own that the prisoner we hold in our power is one whose safety and liberty are of vast importance to–shall we say?–*one* section of the Russian Empire, at the same time, perhaps, it has never struck you that he, in the person of his adherents and officials, holds captive many a one whose life and liberty are also of infinite value. Have you ever heard the name of Dunajewski mentioned before now?"

The old courtier knew it well, the ardent, unforgiving Nihilist, whose capture, together with a score of his comrades, a month ago, had been the triumph of the Third Section. He guessed now what this woman's object was in coming to him. An interchange of prisoners it was to be. Great heavens! What mattered it if the world was populated with thousands of liberated convicts, as long as that one precious life was safe?

"I have here, monsieur," Maria Stefanowna was saying, "a letter which we propose you should lay before your master the Tsar. In it we tell him that his son is in the hands of persons who hold him as hostage under certain conditions. These conditions are–complete pardon for Dunajewski and his comrades now in prison, together with a free pass out of the country. On the day that they have crossed the frontier Nicholas Alexandrovitch will find his prison doors open, and a *fiaker* ready to drive him to his hotel."

The old Count shuddered a little at the thought that he was to be the bearer of these fearful tidings; that he it was who would have to tell the anxious parents that their son was even now a captive within range of an assassin's dagger.

Visions of the terrible revenge the Cæsars were wont to wreak on the messengers of evil news rose before his mind, and he thought of that momentous question the sorely tried mother and father would put to him, "What has thou done with our son?"

"Is that all that is contained in the letter?" he asked, with an effort.

"Not quite all," she said. "In it we repeat to the Tsar what I here solemnly declare to you."

"And that is?"

"That we wish you to remember, monsieur, that you have no cause for the fear that Nicholas Alexandrovitch is in danger of his life. Give us back our comrades, and we will hand you over our hostage as well in health as enforced captivity will allow. But also bear always in mind this one all-important fact, that the other side of the wall, where the Tsarevitch lives, breathes, and sleeps, stands a guardian grim, determined, ever wakeful. He needs nought but some confirmed fear, perhaps the sound of an alien footstep on the stairs, and the dagger even held in his unerring hand will be plunged straightway in the prisoner's heart."

The old courtier bowed his head, and sat for some time mute, horror-stricken. It all seemed like the most terrible nightmare, this daring plot, these fanatics, and he the unjust steward who had betrayed his trust, and now was being, oh! –so cruelly punished for the wrongs he had committed. Who knows? had he been less cowardly, had he trusted to the great system of Russian police, they might have succeeded in dealing the return blow to these miscreants before they had had time to realise that they themselves were in danger. Alas! it was too late to mourn now. He, Lavrovski, the Russian police, ay, the Tsar and Tsaritsa themselves, were in these villains' hands, and nothing could be done to crush them, to torture them, to annihilate this young messenger, who came to him with a smile on her lips and the threat of death in her hands.

He read the letter through that was to be laid before the Tsar, then he looked up at the young figure before him, and vainly tried to read behind the closely drawn veil all that there was of enthusiasm, of eagerness, of mistaken sense of the rights of man.

"Madame," he said at last, "I have no doubt that when your friends sent you to me to-day they knew that my consent to their demands was a foregone conclusion. The hostage you all hold is so precious a one that it is not for me to take vigorous measures unaided, for coercing you into submission. If my young master's life is, as you say, in danger-and whilst he is in your hands I doubt not but that it is-no action of mine shall increase that danger. It is for his Imperial Majesty the Tsar to decide what shall be your fate, for, believe me, a crime such as you have perpetrated will not remain unpunished long. Sooner or later it will bring its own doom, even though you may seemingly obtain your wishes now. I will take your letter to my Imperial master, and he shall decide what course he will wish to pursue."

He had said this with much dignity. Maria Stefanowna rose. There was nothing more for her to do; her self-imposed task was accomplished. Once alone she would feel able to think of it as such, and try to realise whether she had gained a great victory or delivered herself, her father, and her friends, bound hand and foot, into the hands of the enemy.

She rose, and Lavrovski accompanied her to the door, courteous as ever, though in his heart he would have wished to crush this emissary of evil tidings. For some time he sat, his head buried in his hands, then he rang the bell and ordered the Russian valet to pack his valise and bag, and be ready to leave the city by the evening express. The latter, schooled to unquestioning obedience, manifested no surprise, asked for no explanations, and was ready at the time appointed to take the journey to Petersburg with Count Lavrovski.

The old Count started with a heavy heart; the terrible adventure into which the Tsarevitch's impetuosity had led them both was, as he feared, threatening to end tragically, not for the heir to the throne probably-though who could trust these murderous Socialists?–but to himself, the innocent one, who would be made the scapegoat, the whipping-boy, on whom the Imperial wrath would be free to vent itself.

Chapter XVII

ONCE out in the streets Maria Stefanowna breathed freely again, and lifted the heavy veil from her face. She was not afraid of being followed, for she well knew that in one thing at least she had completely succeeded, and that was in so absolutely terrifying that pusillanimous old courtier, that he would think of nothing save of the means of reaching Petersburg in as short a time as possible, and then shifting all responsibility as to the Tsarevitch's safety on to other shoulders.

Before she encountered the members of the brotherhood again, however, Maria Stefanowna wished to be alone with her thoughts. Her resolution to dare this great coup had been taken so suddenly, her one great anxiety as to the best means of preventing the hideous contemplated murder had been so overwhelming, that it never occurred to her to conjecture as to which view her father and the committee would take of her interference in their affairs.

She had acted from motives of justice and honour, consulting only her woman's heart, and knew that certainly the president and most of the older and more temperate men would approve of what she had done.

Probably had they been given time and opportunity to think over the whole matter themselves, they would have desired some such plan as she had carried through herself. But Mirkovitch's powerful speeches, breathing of hatred for the tyrant and all his kindred, impressive and enkindling as they were, carried all their more feeble wills before his strong personality. And they had never paused to think of the hideousness of their crime, but thirsted with Mirkovitch for vengeance when they began to realise that their messenger had somehow failed them.

As to what had actually happened to Iván Volenski, Maria Stefanowna could not conjecture; she dared not think that, perhaps, while she was striving for victory on her side, he should have fallen into the hands of the police, together with all the compromising papers he carried, and they all of them be irretrievably lost, while Dunajewski and the other comrades were made free.

Ah! if that terrible thing had happened, if she was destined to see her father and all her friends arrested and dragged to Petersburg for trial-that trial a mockery-then she would pray to God that the vengeance which had slipped from their grasp they would vent on her, and punish her for her daring interference before she was allowed to witness their sufferings.

In the Franzgasse that night the meeting had been a gloomy, a melancholy one. Twenty-four hours more had elapsed and yet no sign or sound from Volenski. That some terrible mishap had befallen him there was now no room for doubt, and the only hope that remained in the heart of some was the faint one that he had succeeded in destroying the compromising papers ere he allowed them to fall into wrong hands. For this hope they considered they had reasonable cause. The Tsarevitch was still a prisoner in the house in the Heumarkt, and they themselves were still free and unmolested. As for Volenski, much loved and esteemed as he was by all, their thirst for vengeance rose high when they thought of his probable fate.

Dunajewski and his comrades were now hopelessly lost, and Iván, no doubt, would be made to join them. Mirkovitch had said right, they none of them valued their lives and liberties; one and all of those martyrs out there in Moscow would willingly sacrifice both for the great cause, that was to free Russia for ever from the tyranny that places her in the hindmost ranks of civilisation.

Well, at least they should not remain unavenged! The last, lingering hesitation had vanished, the last feeling of honour and chivalry had died away; the refinement, to which Mirkovitch had so sneeringly alluded, was at last effectually smothered in the thirst for the annihilation of him who was one of the hated crew, of him whom at least they held in their power.

No one noticed, as she entered some time after her father, that Maria Stefanowna was paler than usual, that her attentive, respectful attitude was changed to one of courage and determination.

The usual purposeless, wearying questions were put with regard to the possible news from Volenski, the usual conjectures put forward as to his probable fate and that of the compromising papers.

Mirkovitch sat at the head of the table, drumming impatiently with his fingers, anxious evidently to hear the end of these barren conjectures and surmises.

"Too late to think of all that now," he said at last, rising abruptly, unable to control his impatience; "let us to God take it for granted that Dunajewski, Volenski, and the others are lost to us for ever, that on all of us the blow might fall at any hour, any moment, and let us give ourselves over in the meanwhile to the joy that is divine, the joy of vengeance."

"Mirkovitch, you are right," said a member of the committee; "I myself was one of those who wished to attain great ends by gentle means. I see now that we should all have been wiser to listen to your powerful counsels before; we should have saved our much-valued comrade, Volenski, from joining Dunajewski in a fate that we could not avert. There is no news of him to-day, though ten days have elapsed since he left us; he is either dead or a prisoner. I propose that sentence be passed on *our* captive, as, all but too soon, it will be passed on him."

A curious joy illumined Mirkovitch's stern features, a look of triumph flashed across his sunken eyes. His hands clenched, as if he already held in their grip the son of the great tyrant who ruled and oppressed the people; his tall figure seemed to grow even more majestic as he stood there, the prophet of that vengeance which is the Lord's, the vengeance that would bring all the tyrants to their knees, grovelling in abject fear.

The president took no part in the proceedings; his whole being revolted against the blood-thirsty scheme, but he was powerless to withhold the tide of feeling, and therefore remained in implied, if not actual, approval.

Mirkovitch had said, "Let us vote," and most hands were raised to give consent to the terrible deed. But Maria Stefanowna had at last gained sufficient composure, sufficient strength of mind to oppose her woman's personality against this sea of masculine will-power.

Hardly were the words: "You all consent, then?" out of her father's mouth, than she stood up opposite to him--alone, defiant.

"No, father, they do *not* consent."

All heads were turned towards the young girl, whose voice they were so unaccustomed to hear in these assemblies, whose very presence they no doubt had forgotten, or they never would have discussed the dreaded topic before her. She had latterly been so much one of themselves, that her very sex had been forgotten in good-fellowship and *camaraderie*, and none had thought of forbidding her to come to-night when a death-sentence was to be passed, which her woman's ear had no right to hear.

"Maria," said Mirkovitch, somewhat gently, "I am sure all our friends will agree in blaming me severely for allowing you to be here to-night. The harm done, however, cannot now be undone; we must all of us only entreat of your good sense, of your patriotism, not to try to oppose your weak will against what has been decided for the good of the cause, but to endeavour to gather strength, such as is necessary, if you wish to become a useful member of the fraternity. In the meanwhile you must let me take you home. This is, indeed, no place for one so young as you."

She had listened to him somewhat impatiently, though respectfully, since he was her father, but as soon as he paused she resumed:

"My friends, my comrades, my brothers. I have no right, I know, beyond that of friendship, to force you to listen to me, but I know so well what is passing in the minds of you all at this moment. You have none of you paused to think what a dastardly crime it is that you are all meditating ——"

"Maria!" thundered Mirkovitch's imperious voice.

"No, I will not stop, my father, even if you all should decide that my audacity shall be punished with the same assassin's dagger you are even now sharpening for a helpless, defenceless youth."

Mirkovitch had advanced towards his daughter; a dangerous look was in his eyes. Ten pairs of hands interposed to prevent the father from striking that audacious daughter. No one else had spoken, and Maria had repeated: "No, that hideous, that low, dastardly crime will, thank God, never be accomplished."

"And who will prevent it, Maria Stefanowna?" asked Mirkovitch, half wrathfully, half sneeringly.

"I will!" said Maria, and looked round quietly at the enthusiastic faces, all raised hopefully towards her.

Then, while silence fell on all those assembled, while Mirkovitch himself listened awestruck at what her woman's wit had imagined and carried out, she told them, in glowing words, of what she had thought and done, since twenty-four hours ago she first began to realise that these Utopian dreamers were descending the path that leads to dishonour, low, abject, and irretrievable. She told them of her horror when she thought that it had been she who had drawn an unsuspecting youth into a death-trap such as they were preparing for him; told them the misery the thought caused her, that it should be her own father's hand that was destined to strike the cowardly blow.

Then she reminded them of the worthy object they had in view, when first they thought of abducting the young prince; she spoke to them of Dunajewski, of their comrades languishing, so far, in prison.

"Remember," she said, "that that object was a noble one. Why should it ever have been abandoned? Our friend Volenski may have been arrested, stopped, it is true, but we have other means in our power still to save Dunajewski, and not to abandon Iván to his fate."

They did not understand what she was driving at, but still they listened to her glowing words, unwilling to interrupt her. Then she began to tell them of what she had actually accomplished, her interview with Lavrovski, the old courtier's attitude, his confession of impotence, the letter which she had given him to hand over to the Tsar, and which was but a replica of the one Volenski was taking across to Petersburg for them.

It seemed incredible that a young girl, who had seen so little of the world, should have been able to so cooly mature a plan of such wondrous audacity, and having matured it, should have been capable of so successfully carrying it through.

And it was wonderful to see the magical effect of the girl's words on all the gloomy spirits round; the feeling of manhood, of uprightness, temporarily smothered under the dark thoughts of vengeance, struggled for mastery once more; young faces were once more aglow with enthusiasm, that breathed of exalted patriotism and love for their fellow-men.

Mirkovitch only looked grim and sullen still, though every now and then a careful observer would have noticed in his eyes a look of pride for the daughter that had done this deed.

When she had finished a silence fell over them all, but this time it was a silence of happiness, of relief after the oppression of the past twenty-four hours.

The president was the first to break it. He rose with much dignity, and went up to Maria Stefanowna, who still stood, her cheeks aglow, her eyes aflame, watching the result of her words, trembling, yet hopeful.

"Maria Stefanowna," he said simply, "I think I speak the words of all those assembled when I say 'I thank you!'"

These few words seemed to relieve the tension. An enthusiastic vote of thanks was passed to Maria, who now, womanlike, feared she might break down through overmastering emotion.

Harmony seemed restored once more. Mirkovitch only sat smoking grimly and silently; the others were chattering gaily, and Maria was assailed with questions.

"When can we hear from Dunajewski as to whether they have crossed the frontier safely?"

Maria Stefanowna had thought of everything.

"It is to be officially announced in the Fremdenblatt," she said.

"And that very day, Mirkovitch, you will be relieved of your charge."

"I think," he said obstinately, "that all tyrants and their brood are best out of the world altogether. And in the meanwhile," he added, with his usual grimness, "we are to hope, I suppose, that Volenski and our papers are safe."

But they refused to allow their enthusiasm to be damped. Hope reigned supreme in the committee-room in the Franzgasse to-night. The papers could not be in wrong hands, for the Tsarevitch was still a prisoner in the Heumarkt, and they themselves were still free; and if their papers were safe they had, they believed, every reason to hope that their messenger was likewise.

The meeting was prolonged far into the night. Happy conjectures now took the place of the gloomy ones, and Maria Stefanowna was the heroine of the hour. As soon as she felt quite convinced that her plan had been approved of, and that there was no more danger of her father reimposing his dark views upon them, she left them, followed by their cheers and blessings, to pray quietly in her own room that the rest of her plan might turn out as successfully as the beginning.

Far away in a foreign though hospitable land, in a hotel and surrounded by strangers, this same comrade of theirs was hovering between life and death in the throes of an acute brain fever. The strain had been too great; the aching brain refused to bear any further burden. And the compromising papers-the fated candlesticks; where were they now? In whose hands would they fall? Would, after all this plucky fighting, the victory remain in other hands, and if so, would God grant that they were not the hands of deadliest enemies?

Chapter XVIII

IT was about a week later, that Nicholas Alexandrovitch, wearied by long captivity, was surprised late one evening to find on his supper-table a neatly folded silk handkerchief, together with a letter addressed to himself. Any news to a prisoner is always good news. He tore the envelope open with eager alacrity, and read with amazement the following brief communication:

> "If Nicholas Alexandrovitch will securely tie round his face the accompanying hand-kerchief, and allow, without resistance, some persons to lead him out of his present abode into a *fiaker*, he will find himself restored to complete liberty. The persons entrusted to accompany Nicholas Alexandrovitch will wait upon him one hour after midnight."

It would have been more than folly to allow foolish pride to stand in the way of possible escape. The thought that this might be some dangerous trap flashed through his mind, only to be instantly dismissed; had his gaolers wished to do him further bodily harm, or to remove him to some other place of safety, they had every power to do so without the preliminary farce of apprising him of their intentions, or of requesting him to blindfold his own eyes.

One hour after midnight he was ready, the handkerchief tied round his face. He heard the door open and the sound of several footsteps; then he felt his hands taken hold of by some powerful grip, and was led through the room and down the stone stairs he had climbed a fortnight ago with such buoyancy of spirit. Evidently he was under heavy escort, for it seemed to him that someone was walking in front of him and someone behind, whilst on each side a third and fourth guardian held each of his wrists in a relentless grip.

He was helped into a *fiaker*, still blindfold and his wrists still tightly held, and after about a quarter of an hour's drive the vehicle stopped, the doors were opened, and Nicholas Alexandrovitch was helped to alight. It seemed to him that the hold on his wrists slackened, then was released altogether; the next moment he heard the doors of the *fiaker* slammed to, and the vehicle start off at a breathless gallop. He realised that he was free, and alone, and rapidly tore the handkerchief away from his face. He looked round him bewildered. The street in which he was, was long and deserted—a row of houses, all built on the same pattern, not very brilliantly lighted, not a soul in sight, but in the far distance the now fast disappearing *fiaker* a mere speck, which also was soon lost to view.

As if in a dream, and now knowing where he was, the Tsarevitch walked on for a little while at random, hoping to emerge soon on some more busy thoroughfare. Presently he met one or two passers-by, from whom he asked directions as to the best means of finding a vehicle at this hour of the morning, he being a stranager in the city and having lost his way.

The information was given him, and five minutes later Nicholas Alexandrovitch found himself once more in a *fiaker*, this time being driven rapidly in the direction of the Hotel Impérial.

In the vestibule his faithful Russian valet awaited him, whose joy at seeing his young master safe and well seemed unbounded. Behind him stood two or three official-looking personages, who saluted respectfully as the Tsarevitch alighted. Lavrovski was not there, but an elderly man with a decoration in his buttonhole advanced, as Nicholas beckoned to him to follow him to his rooms.

"No doubt, monsieur," said the Tsarevitch, "you are here for the purpose of giving me an explanation, how some miscreants succeeded in keeping the heir to the Russian throne under lock and key for fourteen days, before your minions managed to discover my whereabouts and forced them to let me go free?"

"Your Imperial Highness," replied the old official, "is justly wrathful at what must seem to you our unpardonable negligence, but —- "

"You must have known I had mysteriously disappeared the night of the opera ball."

"Count Lavrovski only thought fit to inform His Majesty that your Imperial Highness was confined to your room with a slight indisposition."

"And —- ?"

"And it was not till four days ago that he arrived at Petersburg bearing the terrible news."

"You were told, of course, at once to set all your staff at work?"

"I was given no orders, your Imperial Highness; and no one, not even I, knows what passed between His Majesty and Count Lavrovski; nor was I officially informed of your Imperial Highness' terrible predicament. The day before yesterday I was ordered to take two of my chief officers with me, and with Stepán, your Imperial Highness' valet, to proceed at once to Vienna, and stay at this hotel under some assumed names, always ready to receive your Imperial Highness whenever you arrived."

"This all seems very mysterious; I cannot understand it. Are you, then, not to attempt to trace the daring abductors of my person?"

"We are only, it seems, to thank Heaven that your Imperial Highness has been once more providentially restored to us. That is all the information I have-officially."

"And privately?"

"Oh! mere conjectures."

"I must hear them."

"I will give them to your Imperial Highness for what they are worth. But it is not often that my long experience as chief of his Majesty's police leads my instinct on a wrong track. Before I started for Vienna, I had in my hand his Majesty's letter, granting a free pardon to the gang of Nihilists, headed by one named Dunajewski, who were waiting condemnation for their last attempt against the very life of our august monarch. The letter was accompanied with a free pass for all of them across the frontier, signed by his Majesty's own hand, and to which I was ordered to affix the official seal."

"And these Nihilists?"

"Were set free that very evening, and under safe escort crossed the frontier in the early hours of last night, when they were handed their passports, and left to go whither they chose."

"Even now I do not quite understand."

"An official telegram was sent from Russia announcing this unparalleled liberation of Nihilist convicts to every Viennese paper, who have published the news this morning."

And the Russian chief of police took from his pocket a copy of the *Fremdenblatt* and one or two other papers, and handed them over to the Tsarevitch.

"Then you think that I was taken as hostage?"

The Russian nodded.

"This is mere supposition on my part," he said.

"The right one, I feel sure, and my liberty was to be the price of that of these ruffians."

"That is why, no doubt, your Imperial Highness, the eyes and hands of the Russian police remained tied —- " Then he added between his teeth, "For the present."

"And Lavrovski?"

The old Russian shrugged his shoulders.

"I will not have a hair of old Lavrovski's head touched," said the Tsarevitch impetuously; "he did enough to prevent my running after this mad adventure. He could do no more."

"He should have communicated with us at once," said the chief of the police resentfully; "we might have caught the villains."

"And probably found me a dead man; no, no, my good Krapotkine, he acted for the best; he believed I had gone on a young man's escapade, and wished to save my reputation. Lavrovski is not to blame."

"No doubt your Imperial Highness has every influence to avert the disgrace from Count Lavrovski's head. In the meanwhile I and my men are ready to escort your Imperial Highness back to Petersburg."

"Like a schoolboy who has been playing truant. Well! I shall be glad to leave this city, with its unpleasant associations. We will start homewards to-night." And Nicholas Alexandrovitch, tired and enervated, dismissed the chief of the police with a smile and a bow.

It had been a curious adventure, and he wondered if he would ever hear the true version of it, or if those who had so daringly planned it would ever come under the far-reaching clutches of the police.

That this was extremely unlikely both he himself and the astute Krapotkine were fully aware when, during the rapid journey back to Petersburg, they discussed the possibility of bringing the miscreants to justice.

The Tsarevitch himself had never as much as set eyes yet on any of his abductors; the only one he had ever seen throughout his captivity had been Maria Stefanowna, of whose face he caught but a mere glimpse in the *fiaker* that eventful night, when she was disguised as the odalisque, and the two or three *moujiks*, purported to be deaf-mute, who had been his servants and guardians in his imprisonment. That, through a description of them made by the Tsarevitch, some faint clue might be obtained was just possible; but Krapotkine well knew that the chances of tracing a man by mere verbal description are excessively remote. As for the house, or even the locality where so exalted a prisoner had lived and breathed for over two weeks, there was no hope of ever arriving at a conclusion as to its whereabouts. The Tsarevitch was a complete stranger in the city, and could not even have told in which direction it lay. The outside of the house he had never seen, nor anything in it, save the two rooms he had inhabited.

The chief of the police bit his moustache in impotent fury, when he realised how magnificently the whole plot had been carried through, and how, in all probability, the daring conspirators would also escape after the great victory they had gained, in the liberation of Dunajewski and his brother Nihilists.

The same night on which their prisoner was once more restored to liberty, at about the same hour, the members of the brotherhood sat once more together in committee, smoking and chatting gaily. The president, who seemed quite restored to his former urbane self, was talking of Maria Stefanowna, whom he regarded as the saviour of them all. All the older men looked up to her as one who had prevented lifelong remorse from haunting the rest of their lives; and the younger ones as the prophetess of their Utopia, who would lead them to victory through her wise counsels and daring deeds.

There was eager expectancy on all the faces round, and many were the glances that stole towards the clock that seemed to be ticking in a provokingly slow way.

Ah! at last! there was the sound of footsteps outside, and soon the door was opened, and four of the comrades, including Mirkovitch, came in. They were greeted with a unanimous cry of inquiry, "Well?"

"Well!" said Mirkovitch, "the last chapter of our sensational novel is closed. Dunajewski and our comrades are by now on their way to England, and Nicholas Alexandrovitch is discussing with Krapotkine the possibility of bringing us all into the clutches of the Third Section."

Derisive laughter, full of gaiety, triumph, and enthusiasm, greeted this suggestion.

"That is an impossibility," they all asserted; "they have not the faintest clue."

They refused to listen to Mirkovitch's threatening speeches, his regrets at the happy escape of one of the tyrant's brood. They were discussing Dunajewski's surprise when he found himself a free man, with a passport, allowing him and his comrades to go whither they chose. One or two of the older members had gone to meet them at Hamburg with money and clothes to enable them to embark for England.

Maria Stefanowna had gone with them. It had been thought wiser that she should be out of the country for a little while, both for her own safety and for that of all her comrades. Let them, out there at Petersburg, do their worst to discover the originators of this great plot so complete in its victory. What could they do when there was no clue?

"None!" said Mirkovitch quietly, "except our papers, which we have entrusted to Volenski, and of which and of our messenger we have not the slightest news."

If his wish was to damp an enthusiasm which he had not kindled, he certainly fully succeeded. It certainly did seem strange that no news of any sort or kind had been heard of the young Pole, since the night when he had announced his departure, under the protection of his Eminence the Cardinal, for the following morning; and nearly a fortnight had elapsed since then.

Though every confidence was still felt in the messenger, there was a curious restlessness–a vague, undefined fear appreciable when his name was mentioned. The president's uneasiness at the topic was also decidedly ominous; but he evidently, though unable to account for Volenski's protracted silence, would not allow the slightest doubt to be cast on his absent young friend's good name.

The ugly word "traitor" had been whispered once or twice, but not in his hearing. The older men believed in some untoward accident to the messenger, but still hoped that the papers were safe.

It would be such a crushing blow, after the great victory, to have to face defeat so complete, so humiliating, with no hope of vengeance, now that their hostage was out of their hands; those papers were so hopelessly compromising, both to them and to those at Petersburg to whom they were addressed, that not one of them could possibly hope to escape.

The president, as usual, tried to reassure them, and to calm the tide of feelings that began to rise high against Volenski.

"Remember," he said, "we must not condemn him unheard. After all, our papers cannot at this moment be in wrong hands, or we should not be sitting here unmolested, and what occurred an hour ago would not have taken place."

That was obviously the case, and all felt perhaps a trifle reassured. Anyhow, it was but waste of time to sit and discuss Volenski's possible movements at this moment. News, good and bad, was bound to reach them sooner or later, that would clear up this mystery.

Some future meeting in a day or two was arranged, and all prepared to leave. As Mirkovitch was about to turn to the door, something in the eyes of the old president made him pause and wait, till they two were left, the sole occupants of the room.

"You know something, Lobkowitz-what is it?"

"Look at this letter I received this morning."

"From Volenski?"

"Read it."

Mirkovitch began reading half aloud:

"CHARING CROSS HOTEL, LONDON.

"MY DEAR LOBKOWITZ,–You will wonder at the place I am writing from, and still more so at what I can possibly be doing there. I have been at death's door, my good friend, owing to a series of the most terrible misfortunes that could befall any man. Do not be alarmed, though the news I am at last able to send you is of a most terrible kind. The papers are out of my possession ––-"

Here a half-suppressed oath escaped Mirkovitch's lips, and his hands clenched themselves over the almost illegible letter, obviously written by a sick man, hardly able to hold the pen.

"For God's sake, read on," said the president, "there is not a moment to be lost."

"The most fatal conglomeration of mishaps" (continued Mirkovitch) "originally deprived me of them, at the very moment when I had placed them in what I considered absolute safety. Since that terrible hour all my energies have been spent in recovering them, for, although I have always known where they were, they always have by some almost diabolical coincidence evaded my grasp at the very moment when my hand was, so to speak, upon them. At last the strain on my brain shattered my health, and I have been thrown on a bed of sickness. Again I say, do not be alarmed. To the best of my belief no mortal eye has, as yet, rested upon our papers, and our secrets are still our own. But I am now too feeble to act alone; I must have help from one of you, and I may want a great deal of money. I dare not ask what happened in

Vienna, if our comrades are free, if, not hearing from me, you have dared to act, or if Nicholas Alexandrovitch still remains a hostage. For God's sake, I beg of you, my friend, not to mistrust me, and, if possible, not to alarm our comrades unnecessarily. All is not lost yet, but I must have your help. Come as soon as you can. —Your friend and comrade,

Iván Stefanovitch Volenski.'"

Mirkovitch did not speak, made no comment; he crushed the letter in his hand, and there was a dark scowl on his face.

The president waited for a while, he knew the fanatic Russian's violent temper; he began to fear for his young sick friend, who already seemed to have suffered so much.

"I cannot go, unfortunately," he said at last, "and there is no one I could trust more completely than you, Mirkovitch."

"Oh! I will go, all right enough," said Mirkovitch, "and take the money, since money is wanted; but," he added fiercely, "let Iván look to himself if our papers fall into wrong hands."

"It was a blunder, at worst, I feel sure," said Lobkowitz; "Iván is no traitor, I pledge you my life as to that."

"I am not accusing him," rejoined the other impatiently, "but the trusted messenger of our brotherhood had no right to blunder."

"Well, we know very little so far; do not let us imagine the worst. He writes hopefully after all."

"I had better start to-night," said Mirkovitch. "Can you let me have the funds? He says much may be wanted; for bribery, I suppose."

"Come and see me at my house before you start, and I will have everything ready for you.... And.... Mirkovitch," he added, "do not condemn unheard. Remember, Iván is young, and has our cause just as much at heart as you have."

"Well, if he has, he certainly has it in a different way," said Mirkovitch as he shook the president's hand, and prepared to leave.

The latter sighed as he tried to read the Russian's thoughts through his deeply sunken eyes, tried to fathom if there lurked some danger there for his young friend. Then, half reassured, he gave Mirkovitch a parting handshake, and watched the old fanatic's figure slowly disappearing down the stairs.

Chapter XIX

"BY ORDER OF THE EXECUTORS OF THE LATE MR. JAMES HUDSON

"MESSRS. PHILLIPS AND PHILLIPS will sell on the premises the whole of the contents of the superb mansion known as 108, Curzon Street, Mayfair, consisting of antique and modern furniture, piano, china, glass, pictures, and a rare and valuable collection of antiquities, gold and silver plate, jewels, etc. The sale will take place on Thursday next, the 12th inst., at eleven o'clock precisely. To view, by cards only, the day prior to and morning of the sale. Cards from Messrs. Gideon, Eyre, and Blackwell, Solicitors, 97, Bedford Row, W.C., or from the Auctioneers."

It was some ten days since Volenski, stricken down by illness, had had enforced rest and captivity in a London hotel, and he now sat convalescent, yet still ailing, bodily and mentally, with that day's *Times*, containing the above announcement, in his hand.

He had now become almost accustomed to his ill-luck, which had been pursuing him so steadily without break or respite, landing him at last on a bed of sickness in a hotel-in a strange land, far from all his friends.

The long-enforced rest the doctor had prescribed for him had enabled him to collect his energies for a final struggle, which he knew was inevitable. Matters, he knew, could not remain as they were. The sacred trust that had been placed in his charge, and which he had so unwittingly betrayed into alien hands, must become his again, if at the cost of the last remnant of energy left in him after so protracted a struggle. Vainly, during the long hours of enforced idleness, he had tried to conjecture where the scene of his next battle would be laid, the decisive battle he would yet have to fight.

And there it was, announced in the columns of *The Times*. The scene would be an auction room, the battle one of money. He had written to Lobkowitz, asking for his help, and now was waiting anxiously to know what the president had decided to do. He believed that Lobkowitz would continue to trust him to the last, and hoped he would not find it necessary to ask the help and counsel of some more determined members of the committee. Volenski felt that they would never forgive, and look upon his blunder as twin-brother to a crime.

In the midst of his reflections the waiter interrupted him, telling him that a gentleman, a foreigner, desired to speak with him.

"Show him up at once," said Volenski eagerly.

He hoped it would be Lobkowitz, longed to grasp his old friend's hand, tell him all he had suffered, and revel in his sympathy. But it was Mirkovitch, sullen, grim, half menacing, who refused to take his hand, and would not sit, but stood firm and silent till Iván had explained, had told him all.

And it was to this stern judge, this man whose unerring hand would inevitably punish the guilty, if guilt there be, that Iván Volenski had to tell the history of his relentless fate.

He told him of the Cardinal's mission, of the Emperor's candlesticks, with the mysterious, hidden receptacles, into which, believing he was acting for the best, he had hidden the compromising papers. Then of the Cardinal's sudden caprice in entrusting these candlesticks into the hands of a friend-a lady. He told him of the robbery at Oderberg, the escape of the thief, his own cautious interview with the chief of the police. He described his fruitless search in Grete Ottlinger's room, his loathsome experience with the coarse woman in the "Kaiser Franz," his interview with Grünebaum, his journey to London, then his visit to Davies; all fruitless, all leading to more disappointments, more hopeless entanglements. Then finally and, worst of all, the crushing of all his hopes at the door of Mr. James Hudson, who, by some fatality in which the superstitious Pole saw the hand of diabolical agency, had died suddenly that very night.

Mirkovitch had listened attentively and silently through this long narrative of misery and struggle. A kinder look had perhaps replaced the habitual grimness of his face, and when Iván paused at last exhausted he drew a chair near the sick man's couch, and said almost gently:

"My poor friend, you must have suffered much."

Iván thanked him with a look, and eagerly grasped the hand the old Socialist now held out towards him.

"I suppose you are quite aware where you committed the great, the only real fault in all this long history of misfortune?" said Mirkovitch at last, still quite kindly.

"You mean that I did not communicate with either Lobkowitz or yourself the moment those candlesticks passed out of my possession?"

Mirkovitch assented.

"Remember, I gathered from the Cardinal's speech that the lady had never touched the one which contained our papers. It was damaged, and in his Eminence's own presence she had packed it up and placed it on one side."

"I noticed, Iván, that you have not told me the name of the lady who had charge of the Emperor's candlesticks, and therefore like yourself has some right to claim them?"

Volenski paused awhile, and then the name came from his lips like a whisper:

"It was Anna Demidoff."

Mirkovitch jumped up; the gentleness, the sympathy he had assumed for a brief space was gone in a moment, and once more there stood the judge, ready to punish and to condemn.

"Iván Stefanovitch Volenski," he said, "you were then content to allow that spy, that agent of our bitterest foes, to have even for an hour our dearest secrets under her roof, close to her very hand, without sweeping her out of our path, or, if you were too faint-hearted, asking those who are strong to clear the way of such a powerful foe?"

Iván did not reply. What could he say? The reproach was true enough, but he had meant well; it was fate that had been too strong. He watched Mirkovitch now as the grim Nihilist paced up and down the narrow room, with thoughts of vengeance written on his stern, rugged face.

"If only the Tsarevitch were under my hands still," he muttered, "all might yet have been saved."

"Then...?" asked Iván eagerly, "Dunajewski —- ?"

"Is in England safely to-day, and the Tsarevitch back in Petersburg."

"I do not understand," said Iván, bewildered. "How, then, were the negotiations conducted?"

"In the simplest way imaginable," said Mirkovitch, "by a woman, my daughter."

"Maria Stefanowna?"

"She, it appears, had some womanish scruples, shared, by the way, by many of our comrades, as to the advisability of doing away with our prisoner as I had proposed all along, and accomplishing by terror what we could not do by diplomacy. When you were not heard of, and it became clear that some untoward fate had reached you, we all voted Nicholas' death sentence.

"She, on her own initiative, thought out the daring plan of making that old fool Lavrovski be the bearer of our manifesto to the Tsar, in exactly the same terms as on the letter you were yourself taking to Taranïew. Without consulting the committee she sought him out, for we had previously ascertained that through sheer terror he had persistently put off communicating with the government at Petersburg. With the dagger, so to speak, at his master's heart, Lavrovski had no chance but to accept, and he became the bearer of our ultimatum. What passed at Petersburg between himself and the authorities we, of course, do not know, but three days ago the official papers announced the liberation of the convicted Nihilist Dunajewski, and his comrades, and their safe conduct across the frontier. Some of our committee met them there with money and clothes, and Maria went with them, as we all thought it would be safer for us all if she stayed in England for a while.

"The evening of the same day the Tsarevitch was led blindfold out of my house in the Heumarkt, and thus was terminated the finest plot ever invented by our great brotherhood."

"Thank God for that," said Iván fervently.

"Curse you for compromising us all and our cause, just after our glorious victory," retorted Mirkovitch savagely, "and curse our folly for trusting you so much."

The young Pole sprang up at the taunt.

"Your trust is not misplaced, Mirkovitch," he said quietly, "and our cause and our comrades are not compromised. Give me the necessary funds, and the right to dispose of them, and I swear to you that three days hence I will hand over our papers safely in your keeping, to act with as you please after that, both with them... and with me."

"You know, then, where the candlesticks are at this moment?" said Mirkovitch, somewhat pacified.

"They are to be sold by auction on Thursday next, and we can buy them easily enough."

"Yes! unless fate or Madame Demidoff interposes."

"Madame Demidoff cannot know where the candlesticks are. Grünebaum was arrested half an hour after I saw him. He is not likely to have betrayed his accomplice in London, and she was bound to lose trace of them."

"You must act as you think best, Iván," said Mirkovitch at last; "as you know, we have ample funds, those of the fraternity; and Lobkowitz has placed them all at your disposal. We must trust you yet so far —- "

And he added after a slight pause:

"After that your life is in our hands."

That Iván knew full well. He knew that if harm came to the brotherhood after this, he would not be allowed to suffer or die with them. He knew that they would brand him as a traitor, disown him, revile him, and that he would die alone in the dark, stricken by the dagger of an avenger, and not be thought worthy the common death of the martyrs.

Mirkovitch handed him over the drafts and money Lobkowitz had given him. It represented a large sum, and Iván took it, feeling easy in his mind. The old Russian left him soon after, and Volenski was left alone and in peace to form what plans were needful. The interview with Mirkovitch had been very stormy, and it needed a strong effort of will to collect his faculties in the last great endeavour to save his comrades and himself from the dire catastrophe.

Obviously the first thing to do was to obtain a card to view the contents of 108, Curzon Street, and ascertain whether the Emperor's candlesticks were included among the objects put up for sale. Having assured himself of that all-important fact, his last move was to go to the auction room on Thursday, and, with the help of the funds placed at his disposal, bid for the candlesticks till they became his property.

The first part of his programme he found very easy of execution; the next morning he obtained a card from Messrs. Gideon, Eyre, and Blackwell, and ascertained that the, to him, ill-fated candlesticks were to be among the objects put up for sale on the following day. So far, so good.

There were a great many people examining the furniture and artistic *bibelots*, of which there were many thousands, but those people were chiefly Jews-dealers probably-and Volenski knew that the sum of money the secret society had placed at his disposal was infinitely beyond what the richest dealer could afford for a single *bibelot*. His mind, therefore, was perfectly at ease as to the result of next day's sale. When he left the house he stopped on the doorstep one moment to light a cigar; at that moment a carriage stopped too. A lady got out with an admission card in her hand, and, without noticing him, brushed past him and walked into the house. It was Madame Demidoff!

As a matter of fact, it had never for one moment entered Volenski's mind that either Madame Demidoff or the Cardinal could, by any possibility, hear of the whereabouts of the missing candlesticks, and the lady's presence there fell upon him like a thunder-bolt. And yet, what more natural than that she should be here? Two weeks had elapsed since the robbery; Grünebaum had in the meanwhile, as Volenski well knew, been denounced by his accomplice. His premises and books must have been searched, the name of his London accomplice discovered, and Madame Demidoff had no doubt acted in precisely the same manner as he, Volenski, had done himself;

and, either through threats or bribery, traced the stolen candlesticks from Davies' shop to the house of Mr. James Hudson.

That her presence there meant the gravest danger to him, Volenski was at once aware. It was absolutely evident now that she had a secret personal interest in the recovery of the candlesticks, or she would never have come to London herself, but sent a clever agent to secure her stolen property.

If she intended to bid for them the next day Volenski felt it would mean the ruin of his hopes. He could now command a very large sum of money in an emergency like the present one, but if report spoke truly, and Madame Demidoff *was* a paid agent of the Russian government, then her credit would be practically unlimited, and the duel between him and her one for life and death.

Oh! for the power to look twenty-four hours ahead to know the worst at once! One moment he thought of inquiring at every hotel in London for Madame Demidoff, and hearing his fate from her own lips, but, apart from the hopelessness of such a task in a city of such magnitude as London, he felt that the lady might look upon this move as a sign of weakness, and, after all, so full of hope is the human heart, there was just a faint possibility yet that Madame Demidoff had not discovered the secret papers. In that case, the moment she recognised Volenski among the bidders, she would retire from the contest in the belief that he was acting for Cardinal d'Orsay. No! all was not yet lost, and Volenski heaved a deep sigh of relief as he thought that to-morrow would, in any case-whether for good or bad-end this terrible suspense, which, except for a few days of blissful unconsciousness, he had had to endure for two mortal weeks.

But what of Madame Demidoff? She, like Volenski, had been enduring tortures of uncer-tainty, fear, doubts, hopes, alternately for the last three weeks. Directly after Grünebaum's arrest she had been communicated with by the police, but, to her horror, failed to discover the candlesticks among the articles seized in the Jew's shop. with great difficulty, and only with the help of a large amount of Russian money, she obtained a private interview with the prisoner, who, deeply revengeful at what he thought was Volenski's treachery, most willingly gave her every clue as to the whereabouts of the missing candlesticks.

A great deal more Russian money was needed to induce Isaac Davies to speak about them again; he felt suspicious, and did not like the mystery that seemed to gather round them. He flatly denied, for a long time, any knowledge of them, and it was only hard bribery that induced him to name the client to whom he had sold the candlesticks.

Like Volenski, Madame Demidoff went to the house of Mr. James Hudson, relying on her own often-tried powers of fascination to induce him to give up what she meant to describe as a compromising letter; and, like Volenski, she felt unutterably hopeless on hearing that Mr. Hudson was dead.

A week after that Madame Demidoff had seen the announcement in *The Times*, and, quite unsuspecting that Volenski was on the same track as herself, felt quite relieved to see that the candlesticks were among the objects put up for sale at 108, Curzon Street. As far as she was concerned it would be a wonderfully easy matter to bid for them, and purchase them at any price.

Chapter XX

A GREAT crowd had already assembled in the dining-room, where the auction was to be held, when Volenski arrived upon the scene.

A number of dealers, mostly Jews, who all seemed to know each other, were quietly arranging among themselves as to which particular lot they each intended to purchase. The sale began punctually at eleven o'clock. Volenski looked round anxiously-the crowd in the room was very dense. He could not see Madame Demidoff. The larger pieces of furniture were first put up, and rapidly knocked down at varying prices to different dealers, who mostly got their purchases very cheaply. The only times that the prices ran at all high were when some unfortunate outsider or private bidder attempted to compete against the clique of dealers, who stood closely packed near the desk of the auctioneer, and hurriedly ran the prices up till the poor, misguided, private bidder retired discomfited.

It was very late in the day when the curios and valuable knick-knacks were at last in their turn put up for sale. Jewellery, gold and silver plate, Egyptian and other antiquities, and at last:

"A pair of unique, gold-mounted, china candlesticks," shouted the auctioneer; "what shall we say, fifty pounds the pair?"

"Guineas," said a voice.

"Sixty," said another.

"Seventy," "Eighty," "Five," came in rapid, successive bids from the various dealers.

In this preliminary skirmish Volenski had not joined. He waited till most bidders had fallen back, knowing full well that it had been arranged previously who should have the last bid for the candlesticks.

But when another voice had said "Ninety," there was a pause, and the auctioneer began his customary:

"Now then, gentlemen. A pair of unique —- "

"One hundred," said Volenski, in a voice he hardly recognised as his own, so excited was it.

"And fifty," came from a nasal tone in the front ranks.

"Two hundred," said Volenski.

"And fifty," said the nasal tones.

"Three hundred," said Volenski, who, having recognised his antagonist as one of the dealers who had purchased a large collection of other things, knew that, though the man might run him up to a pretty stiff price, he would certainly not buy *bibelots* at what might prove a loss to himself. He had therefore quite recovered himself, and his intense excitement was somewhat subsiding; and when the nasal tones said again:

"And fifty,"

"Five hundred pounds," said Volenski quietly.

The owner of the nasal tones thereupon shrugged his shoulders, and looked up at the ceiling, as if he expected it to give him some sign as to what his next course of action should be. He murmured once more, "And fifty," but mechanically and without conviction. And when Volenski said "Six hundred" the nasal tones were heard no more.

"Now then, gentlemen," said the auctioneer, "this pair of unique candlesticks going for the sum of six hundred pounds-six hundred pounds, gentlemen-going —- "

"Seven hundred," came from a musical voice-a lady's.

All heads were turned in the direction whence the voice had come, and curious eyes were scanning the new bidder. Volenski did not turn round; he knew well enough whose voice it was-the soft voice with a *soupçon* of Russian intonation in the pronunciation of the consonants. He had turned deathly pale; his tongue seemed to cleave to the roof of his mouth; his knees began to tremble under him; but in a second all this cowardice was over. Lashing himself into sudden energy, he drew himself bolt upright, and in almost defiant tones shouted to the auctioneer, "One thousand pounds."

"And five hundred," came in equally defiant tones from his fair antagonist in the rear.

"Two thousand," said Volenski.

"And five hundred," was the reply.

"Three thousand," "Four," "Five," "Six," "Ten thousand pounds."

The crowd, breathless, excited, listened and alternately gazed at the two bidders, who from opposite ends of the room, with dry feverish voices, shouted defiance at each other. Everyone felt that there was some mystery here, some tragedy, the last act of which was being enactetd before their eyes.

At this point the auctioneer leant forward, and addressing himself more particularly to Volenski, said:

"Unless some arrangement is very soon entered into I cannot keep all these gentlemen waiting. We shall have to proceed with the sale."

"Do you hold my bid?" said Volenski. "I said 'Ten thousand pounds.'"

"Twenty thousand," said Madame Demidoff quietly, as if she were talking of so many pence.

"Twenty thousand pounds," said the auctioneer, "for a pair of candlesticks. Both this gentleman and this lady are quite unknown to me. I shall have to have some guarantee from both that the money will be paid when the articles are ultimately knocked down, otherwise I must refuse to have the valuable time of these gentlemen taken up any longer. I think some arrangement should be entered into," he repeated again. "In the meanwhile the last bid of twenty thousand holds good."

Volenski was about to make an angry retort, for he was boiling over with suppressed excitement, when he felt a hand gently laid on his arm. He turned like an animal at bay and faced the enemy, who certainly at that moment did not seem very formidable. The enemy was beautifully dressed-all in black; it had dark eyes, which looked almost pleadingly into Volenski's wild ones, as if they meant to read what was passing in his thoughts, and it had a voice which spoke with the softest Russian accent he had ever heard; it had, moreover, a tiny hand, exquisitely gloved, which was resting, like a timid bird, on Volenski's coat-sleeve. At last the enemy spoke.

"Monsieur," it said in Russian, "we seem to be fighting a terribly fierce battle, you and I. Suppose we have a few moments' armistice; will you accept the white flag?"

Volenski gave a faint nod of acquiescence.

"We have, monsieur, you and I, evidently both set our hearts on being possessed of those candlesticks. I wonder if your motive is as pure as my own? Those candlesticks, monsieur, were confided to me by a friend; they were lost while under my charge. I wish to be the one to restore them to him, even if it is to cost me half my fortune."

"Madame," replied Volenski, "I honour your motive, but these candlesticks were originally entrusted to my master, the Cardinal, by his Majesty the Emperor himself. They shall be restored to his Eminence, but it shall be through my hands."

"Ah!" said Madame Demidoff sneeringly, "you wish to claim a reward."

"Yes, madame, that is my intention."

"*Qu'à cela ne tienne!* I will promise you as boundless a reward as his Eminence's munificence could never dream of, if you will grant me this whim."

"Madame, were you to hold in your tiny hand the privy purse of the Shah of Persia I would not give up those candlesticks to you."

"Thirty thousand for that pair of candlesticks," he shouted to the auctioneer, who, with the crowd, was eyeing the antagonists, curiously straining their ears to catch the meaning of their conversation.

"Monsieur," said Madame Demidoff excitedly, "could we not share those candlesticks? *Must* you have them both?"

So extraordinary was this proposal that for a moment Volenski hardly realised its full meaning. He looked half dazed at the fair Russian, who continued eagerly:

"Monsieur, there are two candlesticks there; one is slightly damaged, the other quite whole. I will abandon you the one if you will let me have the other. Thus we shall share the honour and glory of presenting the recovered treasures to his Eminence. I suppose, being the lady, I might have the undamaged, therefore superior, article?"

What was she saying? The undamaged candlestick? He to have the broken one. Why, that was the one that held his papers, and she wished for the other. But then he was saved! saved! He could not speak, he was too excited; but, taking Madame Demidoff's hand, he dragged her through the crowd, who made way for them, to the auctioneer's desk, where the candlesticks were displayed. He said:

"Yes, yes; I agree. You shall have the one, the best one of the two; leave me the broken one—I am satisfied. Why don't you take it? I will pay for them both," he added feverishly, taking a large bundle of bank-notes from his pocket-book and forcing them into the hand of the astonished auctioneer.

But Madame Demidoff had thrown but one glance at the twin candlesticks, then retreated, her eyes nearly starting out of her head with fear and dismay. The candlesticks were twins indeed, for, in the various vicissitudes through which they had passed in the last few weeks, the arm of the undamaged Cupid had, like its fellow, been chipped from the wrist to the elbow.

Madame Demidoff, vainly striving to appear calm, feverishly seized one of the two candlesticks, wildly hoping that luck would favour her in her choice, and left the room, followed by the astonished stare of the spectators, who instinctively made way to allow her to pass with her precious burden.

Volenski, who had not noticed the lady's look of dismay, nor realised the cause of it, only saw what he thought was the identical candlestick that contained his secret papers standing there before his very eyes. Hardly crediting his senses, alternating between fear and hope, he took it up, and carried it away with him.

Chapter XXI

> "MONSIEUR, – I feel sure that the receipt of this letter will cause you no surprise.
>
> "We are in each other's power. Obviously it would not answer either of our purposes to fight out this duel. Shall we exchange our *pièces de conviction*, monsieur, to-night at my hotel-after the walnuts and wine? I dine at 7.30.–Yours,
>
> ANNA DEMIDOFF."

Iván Volenski held the delicately scented little pink note in his hand, and read and reread it till he knew its brief contents by heart. It was such a strange ending to his terrible adventures of the last fortnight, culminating in that fierce struggle under the auctioneer's desk, and Iván, who was not thirty, and was a man before he became a Socialist, thought of that foe whom he had known and dreaded so long, as she stood imploringly by his side, with the tiny, gloved hand resting on his coat-sleeve.

Since that moment he seemed to remember every subsequent event but as a half-distinct dream. He had grasped the candlestick which he believed held the secret papers with a wild feeling of exultation, and carried it home to his hotel. Once there, and his door securely locked, he had touched the hidden spring and seen the papers resting within the depths of the receptacle. With trembling hands he took them out, and his aching eyes travelled over them feverishly.

Oh! the first feeling of nameless horror when he realised that that writing, those papers, were not the ones he had fought for so valiantly, now, after so bitter a struggle; the hopeless sensation of utter despair, that seemed to numb his faculties, and deaden them even to the extent of not realising the contents of the papers he held in his hands!

It was not till fully half an hour afterwards, when he heard Mirkovitch's heavy step on the stairs, that he succeeded in rousing himself from this strange apathy.

The old Socialist had tried Iván's door, but finding it locked, had evidently gone away again. Iván did not want to see him then; he was beginning to think, and think he must alone, in peace, without fear, and with complete calm.

Madame Demidoff, the agent of the Russian government, held the papers of the Socialistic brotherhood. True, but in exchange he, Volenski, held what would brand her before all the world as the spy of the Russian police, and for ever prevent her following that calling again. If made publicly known that her papers had fallen into wrong hands, her government would, as is customary in such cases, disown their agent, and probably wreak vengeance upon her for her carelessness.

Obviously, then, though the brotherhood was at this moment in Madame Demidoff's power, the fair Russian was equally in the power of the brotherhood, and —-

It was at this point of his now calm reflections that the waiter brought Iván the pink, scented note, which had been left at the hotel for M. Volenski, while the bearer waited for an answer.

It was a triumph for Volenski. She had spoken truly; it would not serve either of their purposes to fight out so well-balanced a duel.

> "MADAME, –To-night at 7.30 o'clock I will wait on you as you graciously bid me, and trust that our enmity, after a mutual laying down of arms, will change into friendship over the walnuts and wine.–I am, Madame, your humble and devoted servant,
>
> IVÁN VOLENSKI."

He sent this note down, made a hasty toilet, and still purposely evaded his grim comrade, whom he did not wish to meet till he could lay the fateful papers in his hands.

Chapter XXII

AND that night, in one of the daintily furnished sitting-rooms of Claridge's Hotel, before a gaily blazing fire, a man and a woman sat discussing their late mutual adventures over the hunt after the Emperor's candlesticks. They each had handed over to the other the respective compromising papers, and when that was done each heaved a sigh of relief, and a dainty white hand was stretched out in token of friendship and bond of mutual silence.

And the writer has been told, on the surest authority, that this compact has been most faithfully kept, for Lobkowitz and Mirkovitch never could afterwards induce Iván Volenski to join them in their numberless plots and plans; having handed the fateful papers back safely into the keeping of grim old Mirkovitch, the brotherhood looked to him in vain for help, and he never once joined in their meetings, up the back stairs of the dreary Vienna house; and as for Madame Demidoff, the Russian government had soon to accept her resignation, in view of her approaching marriage.

Last winter, at the brilliant ball given by the Princess Marïonoff, in her palace at St. Petersburg, certainly the most admired among all the belles was Madame Volenski, *née* Demidoff.

No one noticed, however, that she and her husband exchanged a meaning smile as the Princess displayed to her guests a pair of the rarest *vieux Vienne* candlesticks, which it was discreetly whispered had been presented to her by his Eminence the Papal Nuncio himself, on behalf of no less a person than his Catholic and Apostolic Majesty Franz Jozef I.

www.ingramcontent.com/pod-product-compliance
Lightning Source LLC
Chambersburg PA
CBHW071438300726
48976CB00004B/1377